Hardboot Rules

Hardboot Rules

Dag Ryen

Hardboot Rules
© The Helicon Company 2018
All Rights Reserved

Portions of this work have previously appeared in the *New York Times*, the *Lexington Herald-Leader,* the *Louisville Courier-Journal* and the *Thoroughbred Times.*

Lyrics from "Tears on My Pillow," by Bradford and Lewis, reprinted by permission.

Photographs courtesy of the Ryen and LaCour families,
the Keeneland Association and the United States Pony Club.
Book Design: Rebecca Finkel, F + P Graphic Design

ISBN: 978-1-64204-299-3

Queet'n

To all the stoic, excitable, stubborn

and forgiving horses who touched our lives

and moved on to greener pastures.

Foreword

This is a work of fiction, albeit based on events that took place in the late 1950s and early 1960s in and around Lexington, Kentucky, at a time when the horse industry was a dominant component of the culture and lifestyle of the community.

Some of the characters who appear in these pages spring directly from the author's imagination. Whatever resemblance they may have to anyone who lived in or visited Lexington at the time is purely coincidental. Others are real characters whose names have been changed to allow the author a certain creative freedom. Finally, the work pays tribute to a number of real people who were — and in some cases still are — major contributors to the community and its horse-centered activities. Whenever possible, the author has sought to obtain approval for the use of their names and the privilege of chronicling their experiences. Any factual or historical errors resulting from the dramatic reconstruction of the events in which these individuals are presented as participants is solely the responsibility of the author.

Sadly, many of the people whose efforts and wit and knowledge breathe life into these pages are now deceased. It is the author's fervent hope that this work pays them due homage.

Lexington, Kentucky

Acknowledgements

This is a story about the important people in my life, including the little red-headed girl who dismantled my childhood cocoon. It's a story about hope and disappointment, about fragility and perseverance. But most of all, it's a story about what you can learn from horses.

I'll get to the story in a moment. But first I need to set the stage, and try not to bore you with a little family background. Many of us Ryens are blessed with a selective memory. Things that happen to us get conveniently forgotten, and events that didn't happen quite the way we remember become solidly lodged in the gray matter anyway.

This is not an uncommon malady. I've been told dreamers and romantics around the globe suffer from it. At times, it can be more a gift than an ailment. It lends excitement to existence. It prompts those stricken with the condition to ask unusual questions. It makes us wonder. It makes us ask: Is the world we inhabit any less real though it contain a few grains of fiction?

My grandfather was certainly a dreamer. Even as he wheeled the streets of Oslo with his coal cart and trusty draft horse, Valkyrie, he conjured up lots of contentment out of his grimy quotidian toil. His memory created moments totally devoid of soot and dust, experiences stripped of pain, hunger or domestic tension. He scarcely worried about the empty larder or the nagging wife or the five growing children waiting in a cramped fourth floor walk-up. He wasted little time on the general economic malaise in Europe, the recession gripping every corner of the continent. He expended precious little energy on the exasperating complexities of the human condition. He dreamed instead of woodland gatherings, of dancing around bonfires, of lifting wasp-waisted girls high into the starlit sky and opening his lungs to the rich and laughing air of the virgin forest.

My grandfather was also a hardboot. When the grueling twelve-hour day came to an end, he would spend another half hour with Valkyrie, gently currying the Fjording's blonde coat, perhaps joking about unmentionables old lady Karlssen left in her coal bucket, or that 17 kilo sturgeon he almost hooked last winter, or the tram brakeman who provided a welcome twist of snuff as the sun settled behind the ridgeline at Tåsen. My grandfather would speak softly to Valkyrie in the dimly lit, redolent stall, sharing dreams and visions and romances. He would savor these quiet moments with a kindred four-legged spirit for whom recessions and social expectations also meant nothing. Together they inhabited a tactile, sensory world where realists rarely venture.

My grandfather knew the advantages of selective memory: it gives life an edge, it makes experiences sharper, lessons more vivid, reveries

Farfar, ca. 1903

more focused, wisdom more profound. And though Farfar [literally, "father's father" in Norwegian] never knew he was a hardboot, never even knew what a hardboot was, his life was all the grander for following the hardboot rules.

For a while, we tried to get him to visit Bluegrass country where the rules prevailed. But he demurred. He allowed as how he'd only left Norway once, to go fly fishing across the border in Sweden. The catch from that fishing trip had been so puny he didn't see much point in traveling farther. Instead he helped Farmor [you can figure that one out] pack a few belongings, then waved goodbye from the dock, much as he had done ten years earlier when my father, mother, sister and I set sail across the Atlantic.

I came to the Bluegrass as an unfinished kid, beyond toddlering but not yet an independent explorer. I still had a lot of empty spaces left in my selective mind to stow impressions. Most of those holes got filled in the reaches between North and South Elkhorn Creeks, a territory as rich and captivating as the Forest of Arden in Shakespeare's *As You Like It,* as puzzling and intriguing as William Henry Hudson's *Riolama.*

Of course, every childhood creates its own fantasies, mental trappings that stir the imagination. In our most impressionable years, we gather inspiration from the surroundings and create the most wondrous worlds. For some, the baked arroyos of the Southwest provide the catalyst. For others, the moss-carpeted bowers of Acadia. For me, it was Bluegrass country. The lessons learned here, in the rolling meadows, around the hooves of the horses, beneath cascading spring rains, under effete winter suns and sparkling autumn stars, these were the lessons that would shape my life. I came to recognize the importance of these lessons in the summer of my 15th year, the summer we dubbed them the Hardboot Rules.

By 1959, the brood painstakingly raised by my paternal grandparents had been out of the nest for decades. My grandmother figured it was time to make the rounds, to check how everyone was doing, to re-knot the family ties. Besides, she was curious to see what all the fuss was about this fertile Eden in the New World, this "heaven kind of a place," in the words of the pioneer preacher my father so often quoted. So she embarked on the great voyage of her life, her first and only trans-Atlantic journey. And my grandfather was left to his own devices with Farmor far, far away.

I'm sure this was a special treat for Farfar. He could settle back in his threadbare easy chair and reminisce about Valkyrie, about fish caught and fish not caught, about loyal spaniels and a certain wasp-waisted girl who seemed to float in the air and come down like a feather into his calloused, caring hands. My selective memory retains a razor sharp image of those hands. Muscled but not massive, gnarled but gentle, strong enough to swing a maul, sensitive enough to tie an intricate fly. Fingers of a different time, hands of a different era.

My memory of other things may not be as accurate. I can't for the life of me recall what my first grade classroom looked like. Nor can I remember the first time I sat alone on a horse. I've been told it was some-time when I was three or four. But I do remember places from those early days, the barns and tack rooms and haylofts where I spent most of my childhood. I have a vivid image of crawling into a huge metal bin filled with sweet feed and pulling the heavy lid down over me. There I sat blissfully in the darkness, picking tiny cylindrical pellets of crushed oats, molasses and barley from the feed and gobbling them down like candy.

And I remember the people with whom I shared those times. Of course, selective memory being what it is, I may not remember them the way they would prefer to be remembered. In fact, they may not actually have been the way they would prefer to be remembered. So I have to be a little careful about who was watching from where and who did what to whom. Suffice it to say that the events recounted here did happen. They may not have happened to Jack desCognets or to Randy Samuels or to Melissa Turner. There may in fact never have been a Jack desCognets or a Melissa Turner. But I guarantee that everything in these stories fits any reasonable reader's definition of the truth.

I can also guarantee that for every character in these pages, there will be three or four so-called "real" people who will claim to be the models for my musings. And most of them will be at least partly right. A host of acquaintances provided inspiration of some kind or another. Each contributed to the rich and poignant and painful experience of growing up in the Bluegrass. Each deserves to be acknowledged in an appropriate manner.

Nonetheless, some contributed more than others. Or, if you prefer the Orwellian phrasing, some were more equal than others. I've already mentioned Farfar. Next in line would certainly be Far.

Let me hasten to add that I haven't the slightest intention of writing an elaborate family history. I have little patience with storytellers who expect me to be interested in who their great grandmother married under the giant tulip poplar in Knott county. I surely don't want to burden my readers with such trivia. In fact, I created something of a stir once when I told a group of aspiring writers that genealogy was boring. "Unless you only want readers with the same last name, stay away from family history," I suggested. I soon discovered that half the class had just such a project in mind. It was an awkward semester, to say the least.

The trouble with most family history is its alienation from anything remotely profound. Colorful, yes. Touching, maybe. But rarely do genealogical stories scratch the surface of what is intellectually intriguing or historically insightful. I could put to paper a handful of tales about my father's and uncle's escapades with the Norwegian underground during the German occupation. In some small way, that might help explain Europe's brush with self-destruction. Or, I could flesh out the odyssey of a certain forebear, a Mrs. Johanne Cecilie Amalie Falck von Zernikoff, whose 19th century travels took her from Holland to Germany to the Ukraine, back to Germany and then to Norway. And this might tell us something about the roots of European political integration. But that's not what I hope to do at this sitting. Perhaps another time.

With anything worth reading, it is the way of telling that counts most, the intervention of the author, the addition of thoughts and ideas, the woof and warp of reason and argument that create a pattern where writer and reader intersect. Plots and characters are important, but they are merely vehicles. Readers relate to them vicariously, while probing for more meaningful stuff. Wondrous things happen when the themes and images and lessons and insight magically combine to defy temporal limitations. That's when reader and characters and writer come together in a single shared experience. That's when family history becomes literature.

Far, ca. 1934

So, having set the bar sufficiently high, I will proceed with this doomed effort to clear it.

My father was a consummate horseman and a gifted teacher. His role in these episodes was significant, but he was more a facilitator than a participant. He authored some of the hardboot rules, advanced corollaries to others. A man of infinite patience, he was content to let understanding arrive at its own pace. He never rushed a yearling, a student, or a son.

Although Far spent most of his life around horses, he was by no means the definitive hardboot. If the ultimate test of hardbootness is whether one cares more about the animals than anything else, then I believe Far would have failed. His private goals, his creative world distracted him. He nurtured private passions that, however well kept in check, ultimately were as important to him as anything else. He was fascinated with the strange tides of history. He reveled in an ability to charm and amuse others. He entertained dreams of great respect and distant fame. He could spend hours with cardboard and crayon devising elaborate board games about three-day eventing or fox hunting. All these things made him as much a man of society as a man of husbandry.

But horsemanship was his career. For nearly half a century he ran a riding academy; for a quarter century, he taught in the ag college at the university. He once calculated, in our family's somewhat immodest and only slightly unreliable manner, that he had taught 16,000 people how to ride.

He had a reputation as a disciplinarian, a master equestrian of the old school. Indeed, he did not cotton to dissent in his classes. If you were unseated by the beast, you got right back on. No ifs ands buts or pleases. And there was a firmness to his voice, a ring of authority understood better by the horses than their riders.

On the other hand, he was far less rigid than most equine or human charges imagined. He was even-tempered, observant, and quick-witted; his stern commands to green riders were often tinged with whimsy. "Mr. Estill, stay down on your buttocks," he would call out. Or, when the obstreperous Skew bolted for the barn, he would ask rhetorically, "Miss Yates, where are you going?" Under similar circumstances, "Miss Dabney, when will you be rejoining us?"

At the university, Professor Ryen's classes always filled to capacity. Generations of students were drawn by his sense of humor, his continental bonhomie and the academic change of pace his courses offered. Light Horse Husbandry, AG 132, was a popular elective. It could always be counted on as a nicely distracting way of bagging 3 credit-hours. Another source of Professor Ryen's popularity was the conventional wisdom that his courses were easy, that they were "guts," in the vernacular of the time. And it's true that for 15 years he used the exact same final exam for AG 132. Little wonder that copies of it were kept on file in at least a handful of sororities and fraternities. Also little wonder that a disproportionate number of football players signed up for the course.

On a lark, I once took the test. I was a mere 12, a wide-eyed seventh grader with more eagerness than poise. I hadn't attended a single of his lectures, nor read from either of the textbooks he used. But I had spent more than a decade at his boot tops, around the tack rooms and shed rows that were his office, around the hooves and pasterns and fetlocks and hocks that were the living tools of his trade. I figured that would suffice. I knew how much hay and oats to feed a grown horse every day. I knew the origin of the Thoroughbred breed. I knew the basics of neonatal care for a foal.

Far graded the exam and gave me a C+.

At the time, I was more than a little disappointed. An average grade hardly seemed appropriate for the wealth of intuitive knowledge I surely must have exhibited. It would take years before I finally understood the fairness of his assessment. I had only skimmed the surface, offering regurgitated, superficial answers to what ultimately were far more complex questions. Sure, I could keep the animal alive, but could I keep it happy? Could I furnish myself and my steed with contentedness? Did I really know enough? Not quite. For those in his favor, Far always expected more. The basics were fine for college. In life, there would be more to learn.

—•—

A long line of four-footed beasts were crucial to Far's success in teaching. No list of acknowledgements would be complete without them, that smallish herd of horses who carried, charmed, provoked, amused, comforted and taught us through the years. Their names read like a cartoon inventory, evoking larger than life moments of sharing and confrontation: Sergeant (spelled the Norwegian way), White Eagle, Geko, Lieutenant, Silver Jim, Gay Blade, King, Mr. Proof, Trudie Did, Hardy,

Skew, Svart'n, Queet'n, Cub Scout, Fenrik, Viking, Dancer, Go Boy, Honeybun, Colpin. They will make regular appearances in these stories, not always on cue, but reluctantly dutiful in the way of most stable denizens. Their ponderous comings and goings attained a kind of formality. They were the Greek chorus in my childhood drama. They told me through their nickers and neighs and round-eyed glances what they really thought about all this. The mounts were not just backdrop, but commentators. They were the final critics. They would tolerate no deception. It may be fiction, they would say, but it better be true. The herd would be watching.

In time, Far would give me credit for better-than-average understanding of equines. He would take me with him to judge horse shows and actually listen to my opinion. He would put me in the schooling ring with a yearling on a lounge-line and disappear, confident that I knew what I was doing. Occasionally, he would even defer to my opinion about bloodlines. But I would always be the apprentice next to him. There would always be more to learn.

⊣ • ⊢

Part of the required learning also came from Lars Ulrich Hoffman Dornonville de la Cour, the hardest boot of all, the man who taught me and so many others that strength and tenderness are compatible, that the world the equine inhabits is a peaceful world, an ordered world, a world — as Jonathan Swift also recognized — to be emulated.

Lars came to the Bluegrass from Denmark, which, as most of you know, is not far from Norway. The youngest of eight children, he grew up on a manor house called Suppressegaard on the "long" island of Langeland [see how easy these Scandinavian languages are], an estate that had been in the family for untold generations. He grew up surrounded by a raucous menagerie, with nearly every domesticated species represented. From plow horses to dairy cattle to sheep to mules to chickens. I suspect Lars could communicate with all of them by the time he turned 14 or

15, the very age these pages celebrate, the age at which I started taking the hardboot rules to heart. But the rights of older siblings and the love of finer horseflesh brought Lars to Bluegrass country, where he for decades imparted his knowledge and skills to a privileged few.

Listening to him chatter soothingly to a pack of young horses was like learning a new language. The vowel sounds were different. The consonants rumbled out with a strong tinge of the guttural Danish. Still, the sounds remain mellifluous, easy to listen to. It was a pacific language, a language of no threat, a tongue that put the beasts at ease, enticing them to congregate, to bring their soft muzzles to your hand, to share scents as a sign of trust. It is a language we all, hardboots and sandelites alike, should have learned.

⊣ • ⊢

I suspect my grandfather knew this language well, he who could barely scratch out a simple holiday letter in colloquial Norwegian, he whose travels never took him farther than that disappointing fishing hole in Sweden, he whose strong back, gnarled hands and ability to carve enjoyment out of drudgery helped lift an entire family into exciting new worlds. Farfar could read a landscape and communicate with his horse and his hunting dogs with a fluency I will never approach. I envy him that. I may have circled the globe, visited scores of lands and assimilated the vocabularies of a half dozen tongues. But there is one language my grandfather knew better. And he spoke it to those he cared most about, however many legs they may have had.

It is in his honor I undertake to pen these stories. The hardboot rules are only a linguistic representation of skills and senses that Farfar and others like him cultivated from birth. Those who speak that other language will recognize the errors in translation. I trust they will be forgiving.

INTRODUCTION

Rain comes to Bluegrass country in a variety of containers, sometimes in buckets, sometimes watering cans, sometimes washtubs, sometimes thimbles. It trickles down stems of clover and leaves of poa, soaks into auburn handfuls of Maury silt loam and seeps into ubiquitous karst limestone, the mineral-rich tray that Nature has chosen to serve up its nutritious main course of grass. In time, the water collects in a disorganized net of underground rills that carve channels, caverns and sinking streams in the earth's crust. The runnels empty into low-lying creeks and the creeks join tributaries of the Kentucky or Licking River at the start of a long and languid journey to the Gulf of Mexico.

The rain and the sun are seldom far from one another. They take turns basting the countryside, at one moment gentle, at others harsh and inconsiderate. Summers, the sun and rain can get stirred together so smoothly it becomes impossible to separate them. A soaked, glaring blanket settles over the Bluegrass and inhabitants suspend activity in steamy disorientation. Also, there are days when the showers and the sun do a glorious *pas a doble* across the Southern horizon, as they playfully cross paths, silvery billows moving East, the high sun sailing West.

It is a land meant to be grazed, a feast prepared for ungulates, hoofed and otherwise. Through the ages, guests at this lush spread have been enormously varied, ranging from mastodons, giant sloths and mammoths at the close of the last ice age, through centuries of bison and elk, down to the purebred cattle and racehorses that grace the rolling hillsides today.

Generation after generation has relied on its luxuriance. Any mark these beasts make on the land is soon erased by seasons of regrowth.

There is a mix of impermanence and durability here. A dichotomy, a local paradox. The landscape changes constantly. Colors mutate from hour to hour in response to light and water. The seasons shift from oranges to tans to whites to pinks to greens in a succession strikingly bold yet, at times, almost unnoticeable. As the French say, "*La plus ça change...*" The Bluegrass has chosen cyclical permanence as its mantra. The land is forever changing and immutable; its rhythms as constant as they are varied.

—| • |—

Still, thinking back on it, I realize I scarcely noticed the march of seasons past my father's riding stable or our farm on Parker's Mill Road. I had a vague sense of time passing, but a part of me was convinced this was how things always would be — a kid in black riding boots forever running around places permeated with the smell of feed, dappled coats, leather and manure.

Friends and I spent so much time in those barns that we, too, often went unnoticed. We scurried about, lending a hand now and then, grooming, saddle-soaping tack, raking the shed row or sweeping cobwebs. Most days, we took our horses out; twice a week for lessons, other days simply for fun. When the riding was over, we sought refuge in the stable, drawn, not unlike the horses, by the pungent warmth and familiarity of the place. Often as not, neither Far nor the stable boy knew we were there.

From our vantage point in the loft of the stable, Jack desCognets and I could sit and listen to rain beating on the tin roof. Jack was my closest friend at the time. He boarded his horse, Cavalier, at my father's stable and spent two or three afternoons a week there. He was an easygoing friend, bigger than me by a mile and a year older, but not much interested in rank or standing. Ours was an egalitarian friendship.

We made hay forts in the loft, wonderful hiding places, tunnels of darkness surrounded by aromatic cubes of grass. We would build the forts a few days after big flatbeds from Ohio or Michigan unloaded tons of fresh hay. Borrowing oak planks to use as ceiling joists, we would burrow deep into the stack, sliding bales out to create space as we went along. The entrance tunnels could be up to twenty feet, the length of four or five bales. Our inner sanctum, a retreat worthy of the most secretive cabal, would be large enough for two or three conspirators to sit comfortably. We camouflaged the entrance by taking a single flake of hay, retying baling twine around it and fitting it snugly in place.

The old riding academy barn

Impassioned discussions of life's most arcane mysteries took place in those caverns. If they reran the '57 Derby, would General Duke beat Iron Liege? What do dung beetles do with their perfect marbles of manure? Was Roy McMillan as good a shortstop as Peewee Reese? Why do girls giggle so much? These questions — and scores of equally mystifying topics — would be carefully dissected, subjected to flashlit interrogation and rigorous adolescent analysis. We would examine every angle, study every contour. Then, having handled the puzzle long enough to disarm its mystery, we would blithely move along to the next topic.

Jack was especially good at these adversarial proceedings. With phrases and twists picked up from his law-read father, he made the encounters seem austere and meaningful. He was blessed with more than a touch of showmanship, something that came in very handy in competitive riding.

I recall a rainy afternoon in early April, a typical spring day, when the conversation turned to the biggest mystery of all.

The exact words have long since escaped me. But the gist of them hasn't. "Why are we here?" Jack asked, shining the flashlight beam randomly around our refuge.

"You mean here in the fort?" (I could be incredibly dense sometimes.)

"No. I mean, why are we alive? Is there any reason for us to be here? What are we supposed to do with our lives?"

"Oh!" I thought about this problem for a second, not entirely sure what he meant. But a reply finally emerged, as if culled from some future debate class. "By saying supposed to, you're implying there's a code we have to follow, some set of rules, or a higher order that gives us commands. I'm not sure that's the way it is."

[It amuses me today to think how early the seeds of skepticism were sown. And it scares me just a little to see what a tangled field of thistles they've grown into. And yes, we used words like "implying" back in those days. In fact, it makes me shudder to realize how the articulate student has been banished from today's schools. But I digress...]

Jack chewed on my response for a second, then offered this little gem: "Maybe the supposed to comes from inside us."

I had to give him the beauty of that thought. "Maybe. But how can you tell? When does it happen? How will we know?"

"Can't say. Maybe it'll be like love or something. Maybe it just happens and you know."

"So you're saying the reason we're here is to wait for something to happen inside us, some internal signal?" I wasn't sure I was buying this line of reasoning.

"Got any better ideas, Einstein?"

"Not sure. I don't think we have much control over what goes on around us. But you can't sit around waiting for lightning to spell out what to do. You have to enjoy the neat things that happen while you're here." I paused, listening to huge drops of water tapping on the roofing tin. "Besides, it helps to understand why things happen, like why the rain falls. I guess my supposed to has something to do with learning, with figuring out the inherent rules. I feel better when I know why. Maybe I can't change anything, but knowing why makes it more acceptable. So the reason we're here is to try and figure it out. In a strange way, that gives you a sense of control even when you're not controlling anything."

This was my first attempt at a personal philosophy...and one I still for the most part subscribe to.

But back in 1959, Jack shot it right down. "Not everything follows the rules. There are coincidences and random events. There are mysteries, and one of them is that you'll still never really know why you're here," he said.

Someday I would come to recognize the ontology of this argument, this ultimate comeback of the spiritualist. But in 1959 I was still learning.

"That's OK," I shrugged. "I'll try to make the most of it anyway. And the minute I stumble across a set of rules, I'll send them off to you...even if you're too old and senile to read by then."

"Thanks, shorty," Jack scoffed, launching a seed pod through the darkness in the direction of my face. "Always knew I could count on you."

And, for the time being, that was the end of that puzzle. We went on to talk about more practical things, like what we were going to do when we grew up. Jack had visions of being an inventer, someone whose ideas and machines and gadgets would banish work from the human lexicon forever. Not that he was lazy. He simply thought life was too precious to waste on anything as tedious as gainful employment. And the last thing he wanted was to follow in his father's barristerial footsteps.

For my part, I was still in the grow-up-to-be-a-veterinarian stage. I didn't yet suspect that another vocation would call. It hadn't dawned on me that the word games and song lyrics and short stories I scribbled in notebooks were the beginnings of the life-long enterprise that ultimately would constitute my career and occasionally spiral toward obsession.

At the time, Jack and I had no idea how significant our rainy afternoon conversation had been, how appropriate those musings were to the dilemmas and conundrums ahead. Our young imaginations couldn't rival what life really had to offer, but the coming months would begin our education. Sooner than expected, our horizons would be expanded, our understanding of life and love would be enhanced, and we would begin to get an inkling of what set of rules we were supposed to follow.

CHAPTER 1

You learn quickest by doing, but you learn more by watching

Every journey back to the teen years winds up in some way as an exercise in embarrassment. Mine will be no exception. It's humbling to think how little I understood, particularly about gender roles and gender differences. I was inclined to believe that men and women were pretty much alike. I was finding girls more and more attractive, but the fact that they were assembled differently didn't make them a different species. They were prettier, sure. They had softer skin. Their bodies arced and tucked in different places. But those were external, superficial differences. I still had this notion that they behaved and thought and felt pretty much the same as me, that most attitudes and values are common to all men and women.

To that point, the women in my life had been models of reliability. Mom was (according to the admittedly antiquated social ideals of the 1950s) what every mother should be: sweet, caring, pretty and vivacious. She tended to sister's and my needs with love and devotion. She ran the household with efficient domesticity, doing practical things that have since fallen out of favor: sewing clothes, darning socks, stitching name tags into underwear before sending the kids off to camp, saving all manner of paper in huge shopping bags and honoring the holidays with appropriate decorations throughout the house.

Mom was no homebody. She had circles and clubs to attend, benefits to organize. She was a welcome guest at show-and-tell, wearing her colorful native *bunad* and recounting in a lilting Norwegian accent about life on a working Old World farm and hardships during the German occupation. My classmates ate it up. I took it for granted. I figured everybody's mom was equally interesting, equally sweet, equally attentive. I figured that came with the momdom territory.

Vera, my older sister, was also, in my estimation, a paragon of reliability. She could be counted on to torment me. She could be counted on to rat me out. That came with the territory of sisterdom. But if I needed her, she could be counted on, too. She helped with homework, entertained me when I was bored and offered advice whether I asked or not. Even back then, she was a pretty smart cookie. Her two-year head start in the experience department made her a veritable storehouse of worldly wisdom.

They say Vera and I fought a lot when we were kids. They say we pestered and teased each other, wrestled and argued. Funny thing is, I can't remember any of that. Instead, I remember working together on paper maché topo maps. I remember secretively clicking on our radio after lights-out and listening to the nightcap of a Cincinnati Reds twi-night double header. I remember chirping endless rounds of inane children's songs in the back seat of our Chevrolet while touring the blue highways and infinite cornfields of the U.S.A. and memorizing Broadway show tunes and Burma-Shave commercials for later use. I remember mastering the protocol of badminton and croquet on visits to the old country. During interminable family get-togethers in Lillehammer [trust me, it's easy: little hammer] and day-long pastry orgies in Gjøvik [this one's harder; it means something like the inlet of the barking dog] Vera and I added the final cement to our filial bond. As she is wont to say, "There's nothing like a trip to Norway to bring on a good case of ennui."

Throughout our childhood, Vera was my intellectual, artistic, emotional and physical equal. How could any girl be otherwise?

And then there was Farmor.

Had I been paying attention, I would have seen the clues. I would have noticed that Farmor and Farfar traversed life in different vehicles. I would have realized that reality for one was fiction for the other and truth for the other, falsehood for the one.

Farmor, however sweet, remained a remnant of an earlier era. Values inculcated from the 1880s never left her. She believed everything had its place and ought to have the decency to stay there. She wasn't much for ambition or imagination or dream. She assiduously sought to be content with her lot, to find happiness in the meager spread life had laid out for her. She would get her reward in the hereafter.

Farmor could be bossy, especially with respect to household matters, matters of the church and matters of tradition. For her, some things were unalterable and no end of persuasion, argument or flattery could move her. She would shake her head and go on with her knitting, secure in the knowledge that on that topic, she was, and always would be, right. Within the walls of this stubbornness, she failed to see how society was changing, how new opportunities were opening up, how women at last could hope for challenges and accomplishments on a par with their spouses.

"*Det sømmer seg ikke,*" she would say. "It just isn't proper." And that was the end of it. Another form of the spiritualist's ultimate come-back.

It took me years... decades... to comprehend how close-minded Farmor could be. But even if I had figured it out as a kid, I doubt if it would have changed anything. I was just an observer at the time. As Far could have told me, in one of many corollaries to the hardboot rules, "you learn quickest by doing, but you learn more by watching."

That summer my observations were entering a new phase. I had my eye on one of the girls in the Pony Club. It wasn't so much her wavy red hair and deep blue eyes. And it wasn't how cute she looked in jodhpurs and a stock-pinned, sleeveless riding blouse. It was the way she laughed that got to me. She had a warm, ringing laughter that made everyone around her feel like they were part of the fun. She had an infectious smile, too. And once, just once, she had directed that smile at me. Her name was Anna Cerilli.

As far as affairs of the heart went, I was a certified neophyte. Barely fifteen and scarcely been kissed, unless you count games of spin-the-bottle played in basements with a gang of neighborhood acquaintances or soirees at Margaret Hall's dancing school in the old YWCA building downtown. But I was socialized enough to know a few basics. For one, you never let a girl know you were interested. And two, you never let anyone else know how much it hurt to pretend to be disinterested.

⊣ • ⊢

In the safety of our hay fort, Jack and I would sometimes broach questions of romance, usually at his initiative. Jack was a year older and had been on a couple of movie dates with girls from his class at school. He shared, but not too much. Enough to let me know that none of his dates had absconded with more than the tiniest portion of his heart.

"She just couldn't stop talking about other kids in our class," he explained after one unsuccessful cinema outing.

Or, on another occasion: "When you got up close to her, her nose was as crooked as her teeth...and she smelled like library dust."

"What do you think about Anna Cerilli?" I ventured.

"She's OK," Jack said, without a hint of a snicker. "She's kinda cute. Pretty good rider too."

"Yeah," I agreed, thankful for the cover of ambiguity.

"What about her?" Jack asked.

"Oh, nothing."

"What do you mean, nothing?" Jack was fishing, ever so gently.

"It's just that I talked to her the other day," I explained.

"Where?"

"On the phone. She called down at the house. Said she was looking forward to my father's next horse show."

"She doesn't usually come to your Dad's shows."

"I know. She said she talked her folks into letting her sign up for this one."

"Wonder why."

"I don't know," I replied. "Maybe she needs practice before the regional Pony Club rally."

"Naw. She'll make the team easy. Got to be something else."

"Maybe," I nodded, with veiled hopes about what the reason might be.

We scrambled down from the loft before the conversation got too awkward and went to ready our horses. Grabbing a grooming kit from the tack room, I trotted to Viking's stall. He greeted me with his usual ho-hum turn of the head as I slid open the door. I snapped a shank to his halter and began brushing the day's dust and muck from his bay coat.

Viking had been a gift from Far and Mom for my twelfth birthday. He was a simple beast with peculiarities I can appreciate a lot better today. He was a goodhearted gelding, but not particularly brave; he was well mannered, but not particularly obedient. His confirmation was decent enough for a Quarter Horse-Thoroughbred cross. He was stocky, short-coupled and well muscled in the hindquarters. But he had the fine head and ears of his racing forebears.

If nothing else, Viking was a good listener. His ears flicked back and forth in response to noises in the stall. Sometimes I hummed and sometimes I whistled softly. Occasionally I talked to him, inconsequential chatter about weather, sports, other horses, and increasingly about the women in my young life.

There were some activities that Viking enjoyed, and some he could do without. He loved polo, and put his Quarter Horse agility to good use when tracking skimming white balls. He was thick-skinned and hard-headed; a sharp mallet between the ears scarcely fazed him. He also enjoyed hacking, those leisurely rides through the countryside with no particular goal or purpose. He would bob his head from side to side just like his rider, taking in the trees and meadows and birds and lanes and fences of the rural Bluegrass. And he loved being part of the mounted troop Far had established to keep teenaged boys interested in horseback riding. [It's a truism all over the world. Most boys turn thirteen or fourteen and totally lose interest in horses; at exactly the same age, girls get passionate about it. I should have noticed that, too.]

The mounted troop did close order drills, parade formations and tatoos. Far also organized overnight rides to campgrounds along the Kentucky River, nearly twenty miles from the farm along shaded country roads. Viking loved these long, but for the most part leisurely, treks. It gave us both a chance to perfect our talent for observation.

But my steed was not a show jumper. He found it pretty silly to be bounding over barrels or rails or hay bales when you obviously could get

Horse confronts obstacle

to the other side of the obstacle, with a fraction of the effort, by simply going around. He clung stubbornly to the belief that jumping was an activity invented by vision-impaired humans. Only by convincing him, as a rider, that you couldn't see any other way would he reluctantly heave his stocky body over an obstacle.

Since horse shows were scheduled fairly frequently into my adolescent life, Viking's predilections obviously posed a problem. But after two or three years of pitting my stubbornness against his, he finally became convinced that I was indeed blind and that it was preferable to go over the jumps than to argue about better routes. I'm sure he did it for my sake; until the day he died — many years later, of a seriously impacted tooth — he clung to the belief that he was the smarter being.

That odd combination of cockiness and humility was something Viking shared with Farmor. Both were perfectly secure in their understanding of the cosmic order. Yet both were at times quite happy to indulge the rest of the world in its misguided whims. It was a kind of passive-aggressive attitude marked by very benign aggression. And I had come to the realization that it was a pretty nice attribute for a grandparent or four-legged friend.

Viking was a piece of work. He was a blue-collar horse earning his way in a world dominated by aristocrats. The difference was most evident in the dressage ring, where he could master a technically perfect forehand turn, but showed all the suppleness of a delivery van. Style was not his forté, and our career in the show ring was consequently lackluster. But we had some powerful good times, the thrill of the chase across hunt country, unbelievable goals in a close polo match, and quiet moments in the stall with just us blue collar guys in a world dominated by aristocrats, waiting and watching and wondering about the fairness of it all.

CHAPTER II

WORKING HANDS GETS CALLOUSED WHILE IDLE HANDS GETS RICHER

Where other kids had day care and nannies, I had stable boys and farmhands. A platoon of rustic caretakers criss-crossed my childhood, leaving indelible trails, sharing their skills, offering advice, building character.

Jack was around for a lot of this. I'm sure our parents wouldn't have appreciated some of the things we learned from the hired help. Our mastery of four-letter words increased exponentially during afternoons spent in the tack room. And tricks about hiding shoddy work have come in handy for both of us. But for the most part, the knowledge those stable hands imparted was equal to [or a cut above, with apologies to Robert Fulghum] what we learned in kindergarten. I guess it could be called barn smarts.

As you might expect if you've been paying attention, I remember some of the lads more vividly than others, especially ones who lasted longer than a paycheck or two. A couple actually hung around for years, although I have no idea how they got by on the paltry sums Far, and most every farm owner in the area, paid for manual labor and a little horse sense. But stay they did. And listened. And received a pretty fair education. A few of them eventually managed to parlay this experience into real careers.

In a sense, Far and Lars ran a horsemanship school for promising stable hands. The lads would pick up the basics at our farm and stable, working with the cold-blooded and largely docile mounts of the academy, then after a year or two move on to upper level classes with higher strung and immensely more valuable horseflesh at Clovelly Farms. Between them, the two Scandinavian horsemen trained an impressive number of hardboots. Their protégés went on to management at no lesser establishments than Three Chimneys, Calumet, Gainesborough, Tartan Stables, Claiborne, Shadwell and of course Twin Brook Acres — to name but a few of the more prestigious.

The chronology of when the various stable hands moved through my life is a little fuzzy. Bill Shorter must have come before Joe Mangione and Ivar Hjemmen must have come after Allen Kershaw. I'm not completely sure. But I recall that during the spring and summer in question, as the 50s waned, there were two farmhands

Lars

about the place: Randy Samuels and Marshall Fisher. Jack desCognets and I were about to cross over into a new world, a world of painful but haunting sensibilities. And behind us, doing most of the pushing, were Randy and Marshall.

It was Marshall who laid down the first law in the codex that was to become the hardboot rules. He did it quietly and without fanfare in the little red barn on the farm one Saturday morning, probably in early April. Far had just finished a riding class with a group of ladies from town. After the usual post-lesson chat, the matrons strolled off to their cars, gabbing breezily about this and that, walking with short, measured steps that revealed a touch of soreness. One by one, they slid deliberately into the seats of roomy vehicles and drove off. A Cadillac Seville, a Chrysler New Yorker and a Buick station wagon in convoy out the lane.

Marshall glanced briefly in their direction as they left. He dumped the last cart of manure on the muck pile, leaned his wheelbarrow against the wall and paused for a minute staring absently toward the woodlot across the creek. Standing there, he slowly but firmly rubbed his thumbs across the palms of his hands, as if to massage away a lifetime of pain.

"You OK, Marshall?" I asked, stowing my pitchfork, rake and shovel.

He turned in my direction, though in his fashion never quite fixed his gaze on me. "Yessir." He paused, then said softly, "I was just thinking that working hands gets calloused while idle hands gets richer."

No smile crossed Marshall's lined, black face. He stated it as a fact, not a witticism. Then he turned and strode back into the barn to untack the horses.

Marshall was with us for years. He was a good worker, a lanky, sinuous man with strong hands and a resilient back. He knew his way around cropland, could maintain or jerry-rig most farm equipment and was an accomplished carpenter. He was the proverbial jack-of-all-trades. He could replace gaskets in a faucet, restitch a frayed cantel leather, change a diesel fuel filter or go hours on end clearing fence rows with a double-handled scythe.

Marshall lived in Little Texas, one of several rural communities on the west end of town. The inhabitants of Little Texas, Little Georgetown and Fort Springs formed a close-knit clan, an extended family of cousins, aunts, uncles, godparents, grandparents and great grandparents, some of whom were third or fourth generation farmhands whose ancestors had picked hemp, housed tobacco or herded cattle on this same land. When something special needed doing, a water gate or a walnut harvester, for instance, Marshall knew who to call. In those villages resided all manner of know-how and lore accumulated through the ages... They're all gone now.

Most of Marshall's clan lived in tin-roofed shacks along the banks of Cave Run or South Elkhorn Creek. Few had any serious schooling; Marshall was no exception. He spent a few years in the little grade school at Fort Springs, but when they moved classes into town, it got to be too far to travel. Like Farfar, Marshall was never one to wander far from home.

He was invariably kind to me, and treated me with a deference I wouldn't fathom until later in life. Marshall's attitudes about employer

Marshall

and employee, about landowner and farmhand, about Blacks and Whites were linked to decades, even centuries of rural practice.

He was in some ways a defeated man, a man who had surrendered to his particular burden of injustices. He was tireless in his labor, but fatigued in spirit. Nonetheless, he hadn't lost an innate penchant for revelry, an ability to enjoy blues and bumps and good times and high jivin'.

Marshall had his own way of staying happy. He kept his life neatly divided into two compartments: work and freedom. When quitting time came, he would rendezvous with some pals, a flask would appear and the shuckin' and jivin' could begin. That's when his smile, which so rarely appeared at work, would clock in. Marshall's whole face could light up, showing an irregular row of gold-spangled teeth and one soft brown eye surrounded by a shimmering white cowl. Even his damaged eye, the pale blue orb into which little light penetrated, seemed to glimmer faintly.

There was but one woman in Marshall's life, a patient and forgiving soul whose name escapes me. She moved in with him, cooked and cleaned, darned his clothes, and dragged him to church at least once a quarter. After seven years, she quietly and without seeking clearance from anyone, trooped down to the county courthouse to get papers declaring a common law marriage. Faced with her ultimatum, Marshall shrugged and signed on the dotted line, marveling at how quickly time had flown.

Marshall's major downfall was liquor. He was punctual as a cock crow, but had a powerful fondness for strong spirits. Occasionally the excesses of the night before rendered him less than useful on the morning after. He invariably showed up at starting time, but not always completely sober. On those muddled days, Far would send him home with a disappointed shake of the head. The next morning, Marshall would be back, clean and remorseful and eager to make up for lost hours of labor. But the alcohol bug had bit him good. Years later, we would still run across hip flasks of Four Roses hidden in back-forty shrubbery where Marshall would steal off for an afternoon nip.

On at least one occasion, the imbibing had near tragic consequences. One especially hot and muggy day, while Marshall was mowing the steeply sloped front field, he sought solace from the oppressive air in swigs of his favorite bourbon. In time, the brown liquid did its soporific work and the weary Black man was soon fast asleep at the wheel. Unfortunately, there was a tree in his path. The tractor crashed to a shuddering halt against the massive trunk of an old hackberry. Fortunately, there was a tree in his path, or the rig would have lurched over a steep hillside, sending vehicle, bush hog and driver wildly somersaulting hundreds of feet down the hill and into the creek. As it was, Marshall walked sheepishly away with barely a scratch.

"Wouldn't it be nice to be rich?" I prompted Marshall, hoping for a fuller explanation of his proverb.

"Ain't no use wishin' for what won't come. You just learn to be happy wi' the callouses."

⊣ • ⊢

A couple of weeks later, we got a new load of hay delivered on the farm. It was a picture-perfect Saturday morning, bright and cool and quiet. A square-jawed Ford flatbed backed up to the red barn door with bales piled six high in an immaculate pattern. I had just finished cleaning out the lower barn and Marshall was finishing up in the broodmare barn on the hill.

The truck driver hopped down from the cab, twirled around in a light-footed fashion befitting the day and flashed me a winning smile. "Hay for Twin Brook Acres," he declared. He was a young Black man, not many years my elder.

I greeted him in return and scampered up the ladder to the loft. In a shake we set about unloading the truck and before long Marshall joined us. One by one, he pitched the bales through the loft door. One by one, we stacked them off to the side. We worked without talking, finding an easy rhythm. The fifty-pound bundles sailed effortlessly through the crisp spring air, filling the loft with fresh, sweet aroma of clover, bluegrass, timothy and alfalfa. Perspiration beaded on our arms and foreheads, and flecks of grass found residence in the moisture. But our arms and legs and backs bent and swayed smoothly.

At first I didn't notice that my co-worker had started singing. He began softly, as if to himself. Then, gradually, the voice grew stronger, building levels, gaining harmonics until it began to echo inside the loft.

You don't remember me.
But I remember you.
'Twas not so long ago,
You broke my heart in two
Tears on my pillow
Pain in my heart,
Caused by you, you.

If we could start anew,
I wouldn't hesitate.
I'd gladly take you back.
And tempt the hand of fate.
Tears on my pillow,
Pain in my heart,
Caused by you.

It was a glorious voice, belting out the Bradford and Lewis tune with elegance and intensity. It matched our seemingly simple endeavor, imbuing that menial task with unexpected significance. The day and the music and the physical exertion combined to create one of those moments I keep wondering about, an experience more meaningful than true, more portentous than factual. It occurred to me then — a thought that has stayed with me throughout life — that music doesn't exist in a creative vacuum. We experience music within a context that includes other senses, other emotions. No two people hear exactly the same music. Even sitting side by side in a concert hall, we interpret the sounds differently, assign different values to different phrases, different meaning to different passages. We bring different ears to the task and because of that, we are able to make the music our own. We individualize the songs and melodies, insert them into segments of our lives and derive very personalized inspiration from them. It's a wonderful thing. And far too seldom do we take advantage of it.

> *Love is not a gadget,*
> *Love is not a toy.*
> *When you find the one you love,*
> *She'll fill your heart with joy.*

> *Tears on my pillow,*
> *Pain in my heart,*
> *Caused by you, you.*

The singer's name, as it turned out, was not Jerome Anthony Gourdine, but simply Ben. He was "a distant cousin," Marshall said. He allowed as how Ben was blessed with a gift. He had a voice that, like Little Anthony's, could draw the angels down from heaven, Marshall suggested. A voice to soothe that most savage beast of all: the caged human soul. And Ben, like me, was a big fan of the Imperials... which led Marshall to put two and two together. "I got an idea," he mumbled.

The next evening, with the chores barely finished and my boots still on, I hopped with uncommon anticipation into the passenger seat of Ben's Chevy coupe. We drove in Parker's Mill, along the grass median boulevard that once was Versailles Road, across the old Jefferson Street viaduct, hung a left on Georgetown Road and pulled up to the Embers Bar. A piece of blackboard leaning against the wall of the establishment bore an innocuous scrawled announcement:

Tonight and Tomorrow
In Concert
Little Anthony and the Imperials

That neither of us was anywhere near legal drinking age didn't seem to bother anyone in that cramped, smoky bar. That I could scarcely pass for fifteen, much less twenty-one, even unshaven and honorably smudged with Macafee dirt, didn't seem to bother anyone in the muffled din of clinking long-necked beer bottles and spirited laughter. That I was the only white kid within four blocks didn't seem to bother anyone, either. By some prearranged plan, a burly fellow at the door (was he, too, Marshall's cousin?) slipped us in and shuffled us toward the rear of the room. A hundred animated voices filled the place. I couldn't hear a thing above the clamor. But a buxom waitress somehow took Ben's order and reappeared with two dewy bottles. Minutes later, when the show started, the crowd fell quickly silent. Ben and I stood riveted against the back wall, he nursing a tall Budweiser, I sipping a cold Ale81, both of us wide-eyed and amazed as the band, with barely a touch of amplification, wove tendrils of living, growing chords through our brains.

That evening set the standard for musical enjoyment. It was a milestone. My riding boots tapped the floor, my newly calloused fingers snapped, my blonde head nodded amid a sea of African-American jubilance. And way off to one side, at a table littered with dead Indians and pint flasks, sat my concertmaster, his lazy pale eye aglimmer, his gilt-edged teeth on display, his attitude definitely switched to freedom.

CHAPTER III

STOCKINGED FEET
ARE PROBLEM FEET

What makes Bluegrass blue? There is so darned much misinformation about common bluegrass, the luxuriant natural carpet that adorns half the lawns in suburban America, as well as the bulk of central Kentucky. Bluegrass is not named for its leaves, which are always green without a trace of azure, anil, aqua or topaz whether they grow on limestone, granite, sandstone or igneous substrata. The grass is named for its seed heads, which appear during spring and summer when allowed to grow unshorn and unmolested to a natural height of two to three feet.

An un-mown field of seeding *poa pratensis* waving in a July breeze is unmistakably blue. If it appears otherwise, something is wrong in the eye of the beholder, and he or she should consult an opthamologist. In Bluegrass country, as in most of suburban America, the grass is seldom allowed to reach maturity. We've cultivated a taste for manicured pastures as well as lawns. A drive along rural roads in Fayette County is a drive through highly groomed parkland. Those extensive panoramas of green aren't Nature's idea, but ours, century-old evidence about the truth of Thorstein Veblen's theories of the leisure class. It seems that a whole generation of citified Americans is growing up without knowing how blue a stand of bluegrass can be! Let's hope everyone will get a chance to rest a spell someday and savor the bounty nature can provide when we don't mess with it.

Only now, decades later, do I begin to realize how fortunate I was to grow up in those lush pastures and rustic stables, nestled among gently rolling Bluegrass hills where mares and foals grazed languidly, where bullfrogs said goodnight and great horned owls welcomed the day. We had privacy, tranquility and beauty. We also had an inordinate amount of fun.

⊣ • ⊢

One of the chief funmakers was Randy Samuels, the stable boy who worked the riding academy between abortive attempts at getting a business degree from the university. He was a hard worker, a passable horseman, and the kind of cutup that attracted younger kids like green bottle flies to molasses. Randy was always up to something. A consummate prankster, he never failed to make an afternoon memorable. Buckets of water in the summer or snowballs in the winter. Roughhousing year round. Once, he took Jack and me, one by one, and hung us by our boots from the barn rafters. We must have looked like idiots, swaying and cursing in the hallway where Randy threatened to leave us until we behaved or hell froze over, whichever came last.

I finally managed to wiggle out of my riding boots, came crashing to the shed row floor, jumped to my feet in a pique of anger, only to step squarely in a fresh pile of Mr. Proof's oat-studded manure. I hopped quickly aside and looked grimly down at a moist, brown-stained sock. Then I remembered something Far used to say:

"Stockinged feet are problem feet."

It was one of the oldest wives' tales in horsedom: that horses' legs

At the old stables

with white stockings are more susceptible to lameness and other problems. Old-timers at the sales would reject a stockinged horse out of hand. "He'll break down before he gets to the starting gate," they would say.

I doubt if Randy had meant to reinforce this perhaps most misleading of the hardboot rules. But there often seemed to be a fuzzy line between the things that happened while Samuels was there and revelations I would have as a result. The lessons didn't always take root immediately. Sometimes the light bulb clicked on a couple of days later, sometimes it took years. Were I spiritually inclined, I might wonder if Randy functioned as a sort of cosmic courier. Sent by the deities to bring small doses of wisdom to a chosen few. Unwittingly, he brought understanding with him. He doled out understanding, perhaps emptying himself of it, thereby making him more vulnerable than anyone around him.

Another favorite prank of Randy's was bolting the stall door while we were mucking out or grooming a horse. We called it "penning." No amount of pleading would get him to open up, so the only way out of the dilemma was to scale the flat boarded walls of the stall up to the catwalk that ran down the center of the barn from loft spaces at either end, the ones we used to throw hay and straw from. Some of the horses, Sergeant or White Eagle, for instance, would stand perfectly still while you heaved yourself up on them, stood on their backs and muscled yourself up to the loft. More skittish mounts, like Geko or Mr. Proof, weren't much in favor of such shenanigans and retreated to a corner, leaving the captive to make his own escape.

The great thing about penning was reciprocity. The game harkened back to the great Kentucky tradition of dueling. Having been penned once or twice constituted sufficient cause for retribution. But Jack and I faced a Randy who was older, stronger and quicker. We had to close the door on him quickly, before he could react. Usually, that meant sneaking up when he least suspected it, when he was busy getting a string of horses ready for one of Far's classes, for instance. Or, late in the day when he was in a hurry to finish. But Randy was no fool. He was alert to our comings and goings and often stuck a wheelbarrow or tack box in the doorway for extra security. Of course, that made the challenge all the juicier. Jack would create a diversion in a neighboring stall, pretending he had been stepped on, while I sped around a corner, snatched away the tack box and bolted the door. Or, both of us would walk down the hallway, talking about something totally unrelated, casual as can be... You get the picture.

—| • |—

Randy was the kind of person whose life just happened before he could get it in order. He tried many things, was good at most of them, but had trouble making choices. He worked as a bookkeeper for an insurance company, but hated being "penned" in an office from nine to five. He clerked evenings in a liquor store and had one more go at the university, but the store went belly up and Randy's grades went belly down. He finally found a semblance of content at a local feed store, never too far from the smell of livestock, always something heavy to move and enough contact with other people to satisfy his craving for sociability. Last I heard he was assistant manager there.

Among other things, Randy Samuels was a handsome lad. He got his chiseled, lanky good looks from his Italian mother along with a shock of wavy dark hair. His smile was boyish and infectious and his voice had a touch of sand to it. His rootlessness was apparently a gift from his father, who abandoned the family when Randy was eight. But Randy's nomadic bent was emotional in nature, not geographical. He loved life because he felt things and he lived life because the things he felt made him more alive. He was in awe of existence, something I wouldn't even dream of until sophomore year in college. But he was content to remain in the Bluegrass.

Randy was amazement on the hoof. He would look at a string of crows on the telephone wire and wonder what their different caws meant. He would shake his head in delight every time a new kitten adopted the barn. He would look up at the sky on one of those magic summer days with billowy clouds floating by and you just knew he was looking at the different shapes, imagining animals and people, dramas and parables, fables and meaning. He was an amazing youngster... and Jack and I idolized him.

At the time, neither of us could think of a better way to spend our lives than taking care of a string of riding horses while devising another sure-fire prank to pull on Randy Samuels. We fancied ourselves experts on his reactions. "Oh, that one really got him," we would squeal to each other. Or, "Did you see his face?!" We were pretty proud of ourselves, Jack and I. We had studied human nature and mastered it. Randy Samuels was the paragon.

Our self-pride came in for a bit of a tumble that summer. As we turned 15 and 16, we began to notice how women reacted to Randy. At first it was a little weird, a discovery we weren't completely comfortable with. It set us back, made us realize that maybe there was still more to learn about people. But in the end we idolized him even more.

"He's almost like James Dean, only friendlier...and cuter," I once overheard a matron client observe. That kind of shocked me. This was a woman whose grade school kids took lessons from Far and who joined some of her carpool moms for a leisurely Thursday afternoon ride. It threw me because in my cocooned world older women didn't have lascivious thoughts about younger men, and mothers didn't have musings or fantasies beyond their own families. You can see how naive I was.

I shared this problem with Jack. "Does it mean the woman is unhappy when she gushes like that about some young guy?" I asked.

Jack put on his cogitating face. He was already, unwittingly, practicing to be a lawyer. "My guess would be no," he opined. "My guess would be they're just trying to recapture some of their youth."

I chewed on this for a few days, ultimately found it lacking, and finally got up enough courage to pose the question to Farmor, in a slightly disguised version. "Farmor," I began, one evening when she was on the porch swing purling one and purling two in the gloaming and I had just finished a chapter of one of the Jim Kelgaard novels I always seemed to have around. "Farmor, is it sad to get old?" I asked.

Farmor lifted her round face from her knitting and blessed me with one of her beatific smiles. She would have made a great Pope. "*Nei, kjære vene, lillemann.*" It was a Norwegian grandmother's way of saying "get real, you idiot."

"*Livet berikes med hvert år. Under Guds hvelving finnes ikke plass til tristhet,*" she said.

You got that, didn't you. I mean, by now you should have this Norwegian stuff figured out. Well, in case you didn't, it's not too hard. Life gets richer with every passing year, she said. Which was her way of saying that the sadness of middle age is a completely different ache from the sadness of youth. And the disappointment of old age is never a disappointment about what has passed, but about how little remains. And she used that wonderful word "*hvelving,*" meaning the arch of heaven, the firmament, the canopy of God. Under God's canopy there is no room for sadness, she said. This from a peasant woman in her seventies whose limited schooling had taken place in one-room buildings deep in a Norwegian wood and whose favorite poet was the psalmist.

Somehow, what Farmor said made sense even in my more earthly context. We remain who we are. We carry the infant, the child, the youth and the adult with us. The one is but a reflection of the other. So sure, everyone still dreams. Everyone continues to relish the possibilities, imagined or real. Everyone remembers what it was like. Women admire handsome young men and men fantasize over beautiful young women. And thus is experience passed on from generation to generation, the wonder of life acknowledged across the ages.

Farmor and I went on to talk about other things, about family and security and faith and compassion. We never got back to the initial topic, but that didn't matter. Her gentle observation helped complete the glorious picture that was forming.

⊣ • ⊢

Occasionally, when classes were done, the horses weren't too worn out and the sun was still shining, Randy would go riding with us. We'd saddle up Viking and Jack's horse, Cavalier, and Randy would cinch the girth on Skew or Colpin. Our route was almost always the same. We'd hack out around the polo ring, cross the eroded culvert that caught all the spilloff from the airport runway, follow the fence line next to the packing house property, then pick carefully along the narrow trail behind the quarry. We'd break into a trot when Parker's Mill Road came into view, skirt around the public picnic area, canter up to the clump of trees on top of the hill, ease back to a walk and cut down toward the little whisper of a rivulet we called Hidden Creek.

We would rarely talk along this ride. We enjoyed working with the horses, feeling their stride and power and caution and whimsy beneath us. Randy, who was the least accomplished rider in the group, usually brought up the rear. Jack and I traded off the lead. We took the horses through their paces on this two-mile trek in silence and a spirit of shared enjoyment.

For Randy, these rides were a way of learning and a way of giving. He took our relative proficiency in the saddle without embarrassment and occasionally asked for tips on how to be a better rider. Obviously, Jack and I beamed at this opportunity to share our expertise. And that was probably Randy's intention all along.

One Sunday in 1959, we set out on a late afternoon hack. Another warm day in April; the redbuds were in bloom, the elms were leafing out but the locusts were still bare. There were a couple of cars in the picnic area, but most of the weekend crowd had packed up and headed home.

We gave the picnickers wide berth, circling around to the East before we started our long canter up the hill. It was a glorious evening, warm and dry and inviting and the horses seemed to be enjoying the workout as much as their passengers. I was at the lead, bending close to Viking's ear as he leaned into the incline. His hooves beat a muffled, regular rhythm in the spring grass.

About fifty yards from the trees, Viking's ears flickered. I hadn't said anything. I hadn't heard anything. At first I didn't think anything of it. But then my trusty mount slowed and pricked his ears full forward. I looked up ahead and finally saw what was bothering him. There was a car parked behind the trees... this was not in and of itself unusual...but this car was rocking. Side to side on its shocks, a big Buick sedan was rocking along as if marking the beat of some up-tempo ditty.

I pulled Viking back to a trot, but continued up the hill. I could hear Jack and Randy cantering a few yards behind me. And then I heard another noise, a noise that continues to amuse me to this day, a low harmonic moaning. It was an odd sound, a kind of primordial sound. It was an intensely intriguing sound, which I finally recognized as the sound of lovemaking. As we trotted nearer, I raised my hand in signal to the guys behind me: two pumps of the arm and motion forward, the mounted troop's signal to continue trotting.

We swung past the Buick at a full trot in close single file, within twenty feet of the Buick's back seat — doors swung wide open. The harmony of coupled voices rose as we passed and we were treated to a spectacle of bouncing pink roundness and toes dangling in the Spring air. The couple was oblivious to our presence. We whisked by without word or whinny and continued trotting down the trail toward Hidden Creek. Behind us the moaning went on undisturbed, unabated, a song of carnal celebration, a song remarkably stimulating and full of promise.

When we pulled up to let our horses taste the shallow waters of the creek, there ensued, of course, an awkward silence. Jack broke it first, "I have to admit I've never seen that before."

"Me neither," I echoed.

A hint of red crept into Randy's face. "Well don't expect me to explain," he laughed.

"No explanation needed," I shrugged, feeling neither smug nor mature.

"Pretty commonplace, I understand," Jack added with a smirk. "I hear couples wrestle all the time."

"But not usually in the nude," I corrected.

"And not usually so poorly," Randy added.

By the time we got back to the barn, the episode had taken on a certain adolescent and comforting logic. It was one of those intriguing things that happened when Randy was around, an experience deliberately put in our path to prod us a little bit closer to adulthood, a revelation captured most exactly by Randy's parting comment: "And if you think stockinged feet are trouble, just wait til you see unstockinged feet."

CHAPTER IV

THE ONLY PROBLEM
WITH THE HORSE BUSINESS
IS THE PEOPLE BUSINESS

Clients at the riding academy formed a diverse lot. The bulk of them were children of central Kentucky's horse-interested families. At six or seven years old, they came to be initiated into the local tradition of which Far was the acknowledged master. Quite a few adults took lessons, as well. Some wanted to refresh skills acquired as youngsters. Others were starting from scratch, fulfilling promises to themselves that, "One day…" They came in all sizes and ages, from first-graders to octogenarians. There were college students and bankers, tenant farmers, housewives and an Episcopalian bishop. There were college professors and artists, Germans, masons and Texans. Among this host appeared the occasional celebrity. Rock Hudson came to the academy once. So did Annette Funicello. All seeking to tap into the magic of the horse. Sixteen thousand of them, as Far boasted.

Of all the stable hands up through the years, Randy was best at dealing with the public. He favored everyone with a smile, listened intently to their inquiries, provided information in a clear and friendly manner, and always closed with a polite "thank you" or "come back soon."

Naturally, Jack and I believed Randy to be infallible. Nothing could ever rattle him or put the tiniest dent in his fun-loving composure. Randy was impervious to change. Or so we thought.

Despite the variety of the visitors, not many brought any special magic with them to add to the stable's concoction of fun and amazement. There was an eccentric every now and then. Someone to laugh about once they were gone, occasionally someone memorable. But no one shook our adolescent world as much as Melissa Turner.

⊣ • ⊢

Melissa descended on our lives unannounced. She drove up in a gold colored Mercedes roadster, top down even though the sky was overcast and the temperature mild at best. It was the middle of the week, a Tuesday or Wednesday afternoon. I had just walked up to the stable after school and was joking around with Randy. Far was out in the park with his four o'clock class. An ordinary day.

But there was nothing ordinary about Melissa. She stepped out of her sports car with an aura of poise and self-confidence rarely equalled. I remember the scene in detail, the way she raised a gloved hand to realign a wayward curl, the way she cocked her head as she looked around the stable grounds, the way she leaned over the car door to retrieve a riding crop from the back seat. And I can still hear the audible gasp from Randy as she turned toward us.

She was beautiful of course. But that was only part of it. She had an extraordinary air about her, an elegance and a bearing that was matchless. Although I was just a kid, I understood that I was in the presence of someone unusual. I sensed her power mostly through Randy's reaction. He actually gulped.

"I'd like to rent a horse. Would that be possible?" Melissa said as she approached us. A colony of bees could have fed on that voice for a whole summer.

Naturally, Randy had no more time for me, which for some reason I didn't mind. He hurried to get her mount ready, chattering randomly from the stall as he worked, asking whether she lived in town or was just visiting (here for a while), whether she was a student (not anymore), whether she liked her car (as if there could have been any doubt). He forgot the standard questions, the ones Far demanded, about how much experience she had, about whether she was used to hunter seat and English saddles, about whether she could post the trot. But in all fairness, it didn't seem necessary to interrogate her. Melissa's attire spoke for itself. She was immaculately tailored in jodhpurs and a sleeveless cotton blouse. Her cordovan riding boots had the custom-made look, with rolled tops and shanks that tapered gracefully down to her small feet. She had her long blonde hair rolled into a bun and pinned with a gold clasp. The crop she carried was of braided leather and had an engraved gold handle.

She might easily have been one of the dandies who showed up, dressed to the nines for riding without the slightest clue about how to handle a horse. You'd be surprised how often we got that type, the people Far called "all habit and no grip." But Melissa's confidence was apparent. And her attire showed the faint patina of use, a slight smoothing of the kneepad suede, a small crinkle at the instep of the boot. Oh yes, she had been riding before, and don't anyone dare think different.

Randy had regained some of his composure by the time he brought Dancer around to the mounting block. He began reviewing some of the horse's peculiarities. "He's just a little skittish, but he has really smooth gaits and a nice, soft mouth," he said. "And he's been out once earlier today, so he should be relaxed and quiet."

"I appreciate that," Melissa said. Her hand reached out and barely grazed Randy's arm. "Would you give me a leg up,?" she asked.

The mounting block was right beside her. Randy actually had to move Dancer up a step to get away from it. But of course he didn't protest. Nor did I, standing just a few feet away, though I could just as easily have been on Mars for all the two of them cared.

When he lifted her into the saddle, it really looked like she was a feather. Again she touched Randy's bulging forearm in thanks, beatifying him with the briefest smile before she tapped Dancer lightly on the shoulder and headed off at a brisk walk toward the park trail...back erect, heels down, knees in, arms forming a straight line with the reins, hands poised just inches above the withers. Oh yes, Melissa Turner had ridden before.

For the next three quarters of an hour Randy inhabited the body of a stranger. He went to the stable door every five minutes to look for her. He fiddled with water buckets and erased the blackboard. Twice he opened the ledger book to look at where she had written her name. He ran his hands through his hair and pulled a breath mint out of his pocket. And he ignored me.

⊣ • ⊢

A seasoned stablehand, 1958

I went to Viking's stall and began aimlessly running a comb through my steed's thick black mane. For the longest time I pulled at the hairs, feeling the horse's neck give way to the strokes. I tried to sort out the uneasiness I felt, an unfamiliar itch. I knew it wasn't disappointment or pique or jealousy. It was something more benign, aggravating but harmless. It was something akin to impatience.

As I stood ankle deep in straw, surrounded by the simple rustles and clanks and snorts of the herd, I realized my life was changing. Throughout childhood I had been content with the present, happy to go along with whatever came my way, enjoying one carefree day at a time. Suddenly all that changed. Suddenly there was a future, a great unknown filled with trepidation and promise. In one way, I realized it was time to begin taking charge, to create a world of my very own, a life for myself. It was time to tackle adulthood.

I don't really understand why Melissa's and Randy's meeting triggered these thoughts. Admittedly, I was a naive and gullible teenager dealing with a new body chemistry and adolescent fancies. I mean, any red-blooded Norwegian or American boy would have reacted the same. Years later Jack would complain that I had always been "a sucker for a pretty face." He might have added that I was also a sucker for augury. That day, like select others in life, held uncommon promise. It hinted of things to come, of divinations and revelations and awe and ecstasy. It said: "Stay alert; this is only a beginning."

⊣ • ⊢

The banter of children's voices outside signaled Far's return with his class. Randy and I stepped forward to help the students dismount. I took charge of Gay Blade, an American Saddlebred gelding who was one of my favorites. He brushed his head against my shoulder as I looped the reins under his headpiece and through the snaffle ring.

In the background I heard Randy give his report. "A renter came in while you were out."

"Yes, I saw her," Far said. "She seemed to be doing fine." Far always was the master of understatement. You had to be close enough to see the twinkle in his eye to know any different.

⊣ • ⊢

In time, we would learn a great deal about Melissa Turner. We would discover that her father was one of Kentucky's wealthiest merchants, that her grandfather had served in the state senate for twelve years, that she had just graduated from Sweetbriar, that she had two terriers named Lindy and Hop, that she had a pilot's license and her own Cessna, that she hated the beach and loved photography, that her older brother had played tight end at Penn State.

For the next several weeks, Melissa was a regular visitor at the academy. Usually, she would take Dancer or Geko on a long hack in the park. Sometimes she warmed up in the big riding ring, taking her mounts over small jumps or through cavaletti rails. She had kept her own horse at college, she explained once to Jack, who seemed far more comfortable in her presence than I did.

She was sweet and friendly to both of us, treating us as friends, not irritating brats. She never once tousled the hair on our heads.

"I never liked riding in horse shows," she said, adding, "I guess I'm not very competitive."

"Where do you keep your horse now?" Jack asked.

"Oh, I sold her when I graduated."

"You can always buy another one. You could board it here," I suggested, doing my best to promote the family business.

Melissa smiled with only the faintest trace of condescension. "Thanks," she said, "but I'm not sure how long I'll be staying in Lexington." Then she led Geko over to the stable door where Randy stood waiting, and without a word he lifted her effortlessly into the saddle. "Thanks," she purred, then leaned down to ruffle Randy's dark hair before giving Geko a little kick and heading off to the park.

Melissa clearly enjoyed her afternoon rides. She showed up regardless of the weather, always perfectly coifed and perfectly attired. She had a waterproof Turnbridge frock and a plastic cap for her hunting helmet. She had brown gloves and gray gloves and yellow gloves. Whatever the conditions, she came prepared. Upon returning, she always had a positive comment: "That was wonderful!" Or, "How refreshing!" Or once, "What an exciting canter up the long hill!" She gushed about the horses and the scenery and the service.

Nonetheless, she never lingered after her ride was over. And she never came more than a couple of minutes early. She was the most businesslike of customers, keeping her appointments promptly, paying in exact change ($12.50 an hour for renters), and never interfering with the hired help. Before the horse was back in the stall, her sports car would be growling out the drive, leaving a faint trail of dust, hurrying off as if late for its next appointment.

But for a while, we were all content with the time she gave us. We were no dummies. We knew how important the afternoon rides were for her. And we knew it wasn't just the rides that kept her coming.

CHAPTER V

Never drink water. Save it for your horse

I realize some of you leafing through these pages may not have been around horses much. Your exposure to what the French naturalist Le Comte de Buffon (yes — the same family for whom buffoonery is named) once called "the proudest conquest of Man" may be limited to laps around the pony ring at the county fair. Or maybe you remember the old plow horse Uncle Jed kept, mostly for sentimental reasons, back on the homestead in Indiana. Some of you may have admired the majestic creatures from afar, possibly on Sunday drives along tree-canopied back roads in the Bluegrass. But I assume nonetheless that you have a modicum of appreciation for these unique beings, some sense of why "the beast that flies without wings" for centuries has captured the imagination and won the affection of humankind. I assume it's the horses that have brought you this far, not the author's gripping prose. And though you may be harboring a smidgeon of curiosity about what's going to happen to the people introduced in these pages, let me indulge your patience a bit longer. This story is, after all, first and foremost about the horses.

For aeons, men have praised, pampered and paid tribute to their favored steeds. Chinese emperors were buried alongside terra cotta replicas of hundreds of cavalry mounts. No Scythian king or Egyptian pharaoh was laid to rest without a trusted charger by his side. The Greeks attributed supernatural powers to the horse and spoke to their gods through white stallions. Norse kings had their skalds write panegyric eddas in praise of horses.

As everyone learned in grade school, horses were brought to the New World by European explorers in the 16th century. Cortez' favorite steed, El Morzillo, was such a splendid animal that he shook Inca civilization to its roots. The great empire builders of South America had never seen such creatures, never experienced such serene and powerful, swift and courageous apparitions. They concluded that the chargers of the conquistadors were nothing less than a special race of gods, and proceeded to build a statue in homage to the nonparei among them, El Morzillo.

[Actually, what we learned about horses in grade school is mostly wrong. Actually, quite a bit of what we learned in grade school is wrong. But I digress...]

Spanish horses were not the first equines to roam the Western Hemisphere. The earliest forerunner of today's horse, Eohippus, inhabited large areas in and around the Mississippi Valley, including what would become the Bluegrass Plateau, more than fifty million years ago. This was the Eocene epoch, a time long before humans rose up on their hind legs and began a determined quest to subjugate the planet and all its beings. Though much smaller than today's equines, this "horse of the dawn" grazed prehistoric plains and savannah woodlands in large herds, and their fossilized remains, common from Louisiana to Montana, show the distinctive features that characterize today's animal: slender limbs with extended tendons and toes structured to carry weight in movement.

Eohippus disappeared mysteriously from earth...as surely we all shall...but its successors lived on in the Old World. Evolving through a series of species, the first example of the modern horse, *equus caballus,* appeared some fifty to a hundred thousand years ago in central Asia. Known as Przewalski's horse in honor of the Polish scientist who first described it, this sturdy, brownish animal was the forerunner of Chinese and Mongol war breeds that became the scourge of Asia and Europe during the conquests of Ghengis Khan.

Sometimes when I looked at Viking, I could see Przewalski-ness in him. He had the sturdiness and bulk of this ancestor. There was also a certain sang-froid, a primitive willingness to charge into uncertainty (unless there was a jump in the way, of course), a nonchalance about danger that could be interpreted either as stubbornness or pure stupidity. That one strange characteristic, that apparently dumb but at the same time incredibly courageous demeanor, may be the key to man's affinity for horses. They do our bidding without much question. We may wonder about the wisdom of a certain course of action, they never do. They can be supremely decisive. It's not so much trust that drives them as duty. And the duty they perform is not to honor their masters. In performing, they honor their own race instead.

Little wonder horses have occupied a special place in the labors, wars, pleasures and lives of man. What other animal can you think of so often recalled in speech, legend and statuary? We remember individual horses by name. What other animal can make that claim? Only one lioness: Elsa. An elephant or two. (You can't count Babar, since he was fictional... or can you?) Maybe a dozen or so dogs. But hundreds of horses have made their way into our history books: Bucephalus, the charger of Alexander the Great; Incitatus, the horse that Caligula appointed to the Roman Senate; Richard II's steed Roan Barbery, made famous by Shakespeare; Copenhagen, the Duke of Wellington's horse, which was buried with full military honors; Marengo, the white stallion Napoleon rode into his defeat at Waterloo; Traveler, Gen. Robert E. Lee's gray horse; Bess, the favorite mount of rebel raider John Hunt Morgan; Comanche, the sole survivor of the Battle of the Little Bighorn, Svart'n, the black darling of Kob Ryen's Riding Academy. Not to mention all the storied racing champions of modern times, the Citations and Whirlaways and Man o' Wars. They have always been with us, these snorting giants, doing our bidding, with scarcely a complaint.

Without them, the Bluegrass would have been a sad, desolate place.

—⊣ • ⊢—

April slipped into May. A perfect Derby Day arrived and we sat in the library, sipping mint juleps. Or rather, I sipped on a small mint julep while Far enjoyed his customary Mark and Seven. "Don't like mint juleps," Far said. "They've got water in them. Never drink water, save it for your horse," he advised. I suspect he was led to that conviction by W.C. Fields, one of his favorite comedians. Far also loved quoting the opening lines from *Around the World in Eighty Days*, where the stodgy English gentleman complains to his clubmates about ice in the drinks. "Learned it from some Yankee, I dare say." A simple waste of water, Far agreed.

We followed the Derby festivities on the radio, since Far as a matter of principle still refused to buy a television. "It would only interfere with your homework," was his justification. It wouldn't be long before he tossed that principle aside in favor of *Gunsmoke*, *Lawrence Welk*, and the *NBC News Hour*.

The Derby that year didn't promise to offer much excitement. Sword Dancer was the odds-on favorite, and most folks tuned in just to see how much he would win by. But, as is often the case in the Sport of Kings, the favorite was taken down. We listened intently as the upstart Tomy Lee and Sword Dancer bumped and battled down the stretch, with Bill Shoemaker finally whipping Tomy Lee to a whisker-thin victory in one of the most controversial Kentucky Derbies ever. A complaint was lodged, and stewards discussed the inquiry for almost twenty minutes before disallowing the inquiry.

It was a big victory for Tomy Lee, who was a rangy colt with an up-and-down career. The horse looked the part, but he didn't always fire. Some touts blamed his troubles on four white legs. Far just shook his head.

At the stable the following morning, Jack and I discussed the controversy.

"Looked to me like Sword Dancer got bumped at least twice," Jack offered.

"Really."

"Yeah. Didn't you see it?"

"No. We were listening on the radio."

"Oh, yeah. I forgot your Dad won't get a television."

I chuckled at this common complaint among my friends. "It's OK. The radio show was pretty suspenseful. The announcer seemed to agree with you."

"What did you think, Marshall?" Jack turned to our farm hand who was covering stable duties that day.

"I think that bay colt deserve everything he got," Marshall commented. "But I'm mostly always for the underdog."

"Sword Dancer will come back in the Preakness," Jack predicted.

"We'll see," Marshall smiled. "Always somebody itchin' for an upset"

"You think so?"

"We'll just see," Marshall repeated before returning to his duties.

⊢ • ⊣

It was a quiet day at the stables. The clear Saturday weather had given way to a humid haze as Gulf moisture crept into the Bluegrass. The forecasters were predicting showers by afternoon. To beat the rain, Jack and I decided to go for an early ride and began tacking up the horses. It was shaping up to be a pretty ordinary day. But stables have their way of throwing surprises at you.

I was inside Viking's stall, fitting his saddle on the saddle blanket, when I heard the growl of a familiar Mercedes pull up outside the stable, followed by soft footsteps.

"Hello? Randy?" Melissa called from the entrance.

"Sorry, Miss," Marshall came around the corner. "He's not here today. Anything I can do?"

"Oh." Her surprise and disappointment were audible. "I just thought I'd go for a ride."

"Yes, ma'am. Them boys 'bout to go out. Want to join them?" Marshall asked.

I stuck my head out the door and waved, both pleased and unnerved at Marshall's suggestion.

Melissa lifted her gloved hand half-heartedly and paused, seeming to weigh her options. "I think I'll just go out alone," she said finally. "I'm not very good company today."

"Yes, ma'am," Marshall acknowledged. "I'll get Dancer ready in a flash."

I ducked back into the stall and continued cinching Viking's girth, trying to ignore the fact that I was a little miffed. She wasn't exactly snubbing us. But it wasn't like we hadn't gotten to know her, either. On the other hand, why in the world would she want to ride with two social greenhorns like Jack and me.

I tugged mightily on the leather straps while leaning into Viking's barrel. Unfortunately, he was one of those horses that blew up their lungs when you tried to put the saddle on, then exhaled when the girth had been secured. It was an understandable trait. Pretty smart, really. Made the saddle more comfortable for the horse, if a bit more hazardous for the rider. Sometimes today, I feel the same way about car seat belts.

I heaved a bit harder and felt the buckle tongue pop into its appropriate hole. Then I realized that Melissa was standing in the open stall door.

"He's a nice horse," she began. "He's yours, isn't he?"

"Uh huh," I mumbled, a little out of breath.

"Do you show him a lot?"

I had to chuckle in spite of myself. "Not really. He's not much of a show horse. Just a good friend. He likes trail riding."

"Sounds like me," Melissa commented, as much to herself as to me or my horse.

"I would have thought you did a lot of show riding."

"I used to. When I was a little girl. Then I got tired of all the fuss and pretention. And I developed other interests."

I leaned against Viking's shoulder and looked at her for a minute. Framed in the light from the hallway, she formed almost an unreal silhouette, graceful and whispy, as if she could dissipate any moment. But definitely not a little girl anymore.

There was a awkward silence that I worsened with my next comment. "I'm sorry you won't be riding with us," I said.

"Oh, I'm really sorry," she replied quickly. "I didn't mean to be rude or anything. It would be nice to join Jack and you sometime. I'm just kind of in a bad mood today, and I hoped Randy would be here so I could talk to him."

"He has the day off today. Because of the academy horse show next weekend."

She nodded. "Maybe I could leave him a note," she murmured, mostly to herself.

"You could call him. We've got his number in the office."

"No, I don't want to do that,"

"Or I could give him a message."

Even with the backlit doorway, I could make out her broad smile. "It's not so much a message," she said. "But you can certainly tell him I want to talk to him."

"OK," I laughed back. "I'll see him tomorrow after school."

"Thanks," Melissa smiled, backing into the shed row, "Thanks a bunch. He's lucky to have such good friends."

She was gone before I could come up with any reply, any ploy to keep the conversation going. Instead, I was left with my four-footed bay wondering what she wanted to talk to Randy about and not really wondering because I figured I had a pretty good idea, but still wondering why she couldn't just call him, and puzzled about how difficult some things seemed to be when they ought to be so easy.

"You ready, yet, Shorty!" Jack appeared outside the doorway, already mounted. "Ready or not, we're heading out."

Ready as I'll ever be, I thought to myself. Melissa was nowhere in sight as we left the barn.

⊣ • ⊢

We took off at our normal quick trot down to the park and past the quarry, moving quickly around the picnic area. Then, instead of heading up the hill, we slowed to a walk along the trail parallel to Parker's Mill.

The air was bleary and bright at the same time, with sunlight hitting the moisture and exploding in a million directions. It seemed filled with curiosity and questions. I hacked along quietly, thinking about my own puzzles.

We hadn't gotten more than a couple of hundred feet past the picnic area when we came on a large gathering of people. Some were already blocking the trail, others just crossing the road. My first guess was that something had happened, that there had been an accident. Had Melissa fallen and hurt herself? I gulped and banished that thought. Then I took a closer look at the throng. Many were wearing white robes; others were dressed in Sunday finest. This was no random gathering, it was a group with a purpose.

Jack reined Cavalier to a stop next to a clump of ash trees and I pulled up beside him. We were on a small rise just opposite the country store that sat in the middle of Little Georgetown. But the people weren't coming from the store. They were coming from the little country church, Bethany Baptist, that sat adjacent to it. And they were gathering around a small pond just behind the culvert where Hidden Creek flowed under the road.

"What's going on?" Jack wondered aloud.

At that point, two of the robed men waded into the pond. They were carrying what looked like tall walking sticks and they began to beat the surface of the water, moving systematically from one end of the impoundment to the other. They worked the water like rug-beaters, slapping their sticks first one way then the other.

"What are they doing that for?" Jack asked.

Moments later, it became obvious. At the upstream end of the pond, critters suddenly emerged. First a weasel, then a couple of muskrats.

Baptism pond

Frogs began hopping out on both sides. And then we spotted the snakes, six or seven that slithered out of the water and slime and sought refuge in tall grass along the banks.

"Wow," we marveled in unison.

"Golly," we repeated.

"It must be a baptism" Jack said.

For some reason, we couldn't move. We didn't want to move. The scene mesmerized us. It exuded a kind of primal force, some rustic artlessness that seemed intensely appropriate. The area was bathed in a white mist that enveloped us, held us in place and made us part of the congregation.

Soon some thirty or forty souls were gathered by the pond. They closed ranks, and offered preliminary chants before the preacher, holding what looked like a well-worn Bible waded into the center of the pond. Voices were raised in song, a rich jubilant hymn that swelled and ebbed and mixed with the air in eddies of light and sound. Then, one by one, celebrants joined him and the deacons in the now muddied waters, to be immersed and blessed in turn.

Each white-robed celebrant walked calmly up to the preacher, who placed his hand on the candidate's head and slowly, but firmly shoved it down until nothing remained above the surface except billowing mounds of white robe bobbing on the water. The preacher held them there for what seemed like an eternity, as he sang out in praise. Seconds passed… minutes, with only bubbles boiling up from the opaque pond. Then, at last, he would release the celebrant, who would burst out of foam, sputtering and shouting, now draped in an off-white garment, only to be greeted by a chorus of halleluias from the congregation.

On the rise, only a hundred feet or so away, we watched quietly. The critters stayed hidden in the grass. Occasionally, a member of the congregation would glance in our direction. One even waved for us to join them. I waved back, but didn't budge. It was like a scene from a movie, and I was much more comfortable in the audience.

⊣ • ⊢

We waited until the entire ceremony was finished, half an hour or more, letting our horses graze on loose reins while we sat transfixed watching an event that was so common to some and so unfamiliar to us. On the leisurely ride back to the barn, I realized how often we place artificial barriers between us. The black congregation at Bethany and the white congregation at Faith Lutheran did some things in totally different ways. And sometimes that made us uncomfortable with each other. But if we only got used to it, it wouldn't matter.

I couldn't have articulated it that day, but I knew deep inside that the same thing was happening to Randy and Melissa. They were fighting their way through artificial barriers, trying to get used to each other's habits. In my adolescent fervor, I saw that as an exciting challenge.

⊣ • ⊢

Some of the awe had worn off by the time we neared the stable. And a few light drops of rain were penetrating the mist. We picked up the pace to hurry inside. But before rounding the riding ring, Jack suddenly asked, as if he had been pondering the question for some time, "Do you think they sometimes end up drinking some of that water?"

I laughed out loud and shot back, "Not a chance. Those are farm folks. They never drink water. They save it for their horses."

CHAPTER VI

OUT OF THE SADDLE AND ONTO THE GROUND? BACK IN THE SADDLE WILL TURN THINGS AROUND

Getting the horses ready for one of Far's horse shows was a week-long task. Every horse was soaped down and rinsed. Stars, stripes, socks and stockings were carefully scrubbed to remove any trace of manure or grass stain. Hooves were trimmed and painted. Manes, tails and forelocks were pulled and combed. Some were actually braided, especially if the beast in question had a special admirer with an hour or so of extra time. Tack was saddle-soaped and name tags polished. All this special attention gradually made its way into the horses' heads. As the week wore on they became more alert, more curious, sensing that something was afoot.

The place got a fix-up, too. Marshall mowed every field and re-nailed each sagging fence plank. Randy slapped paint on stall doors and raked out new gravel in the parking lot. Afternoons after school, Jack and I helped distribute fence numbers for the cross-country course.

Mom was in charge of trophies and ribbons from Miller & Woodward or Paul DeLott, and refreshments, which usually consisted of a big coffee urn by the barn door and soda pop in a tub of ice. Farmor helped, too, by stitching a big welcome banner to hang over the main drive.

The shows at the Riding Academy were low-key affairs that nonetheless had a carnival air about them. They were primarily a sort of recital for

Far's students, but through the years other riders found them useful as tune-ups before bigger shows like the Junior League or the Block and Bridle Club. In the early years, Far ran the event from the airport stable, barking directions through a hand-held megaphone like a circus ring-master. Later, the shows were moved across the road to the farm, allowing separate areas for equitation, stadium jumping and cross-country.

The show always began at 9:00 o'clock sharp. Far made a big point of being on time. He was so punctual it bordered on the punctilious. The first classes were equitation for different age groups, 6 years to seniors. There would be a break for lunch around 11:00. And then the equitation over jumps, green hunter and cross-country in the afternoon.

The spring show of 1959 took place under a brilliantly blue May sky. Trailers began pulling in soon after daybreak. By eight, a dozen of them were clustered on the grassy lawn between the house and lower barn. Cars parked head-on around the show ring, giving parents, friends and other spectators a front row view. All around, people led chestnuts, bays, roans, grays and an occasional appaloosa in their Saturday go-to-meeting finery. New horses emerged from trailers decked out in colorful blankets and crisp bandages, and were taken for a stroll to shake off

Equitation class

trailer stiffness. Riders in formal habit milled around the barns, fussing over tack or glancing nervously at arriving competition. Parents offered encouragement, cajolement or threat, anything to get their charges, human and equine, organized and motivated.

This particular show, held sometime just before school was out, stands out in my memory for a number of reasons. The most obvious is my connection to several of the participants, as you will soon discover. It was also the only time Farmor watched me compete. And, not least, it was an event blessed with absolutely immaculate weather. A quiet midnight shower had softened the lush grass and settled the dust. A mild front eased in from the west-northwest, and the sun rose quickly to burn off the morning dew and then beam benignly through the clear air. The magnolia tree in front of the house seemed to explode with brilliant purple-white flowers. Mom's irises and even a few lingering jonquils basked in the sunlight. Boxes of geraniums around the show ring perked up proudly, and all around the farm, wild rose bushes were sprinkled with white blossoms.

As a kid, I couldn't tell a daffodil from a goldenrod. But today, when I cull them from memory, they stand forth so clearly I can pull out my flower guide and identify every bloom.

Another reason I remember this show so vividly is because the judge was the aptly named Stoney Johnson, a hardboot if ever there was one and a legend to every young rider in Central Kentucky at the time. Ms. Johnson had a reputation to match Far's, only she never sugarcoated anything. She could outbark a Jack Russel terrier and outglare a hoot owl. But she knew her horses and she knew riding and she was on the selection team for the Pony Club. We were all a good bit in awe of her, which seems ironic now, because she really was a wonderfully kind and caring person. Unfortunately, this kindness rarely radiated on anyone sitting in a saddle.

Far had outside judges come in for the shows to provide some objectivity, sometimes from as far away as Pennsylvania or Alabama. Many of the competitors didn't have their own horses and had to settle for what the academy could offer — on a first-come, first-served basis. That was great for the early birds who got Silver Jim or Gay Blade. Far had taken Silver Jim to the U.S. Olympic Trials and walked away with the dressage competition back in the days before lines between professional and amateur athletics were erased completely.

The first-come, first-served rule was not so great for clients stuck with Mr. Proof in an equitation class (after four years on the race track, he simply would not take the right lead at the canter), or King in a class over jumps (he did Viking one worse in the jumping department). Needless to say, at Kob Ryen's Riding Academy, Vera and I had to make do with whatever was left over.

As I recall, Far normally had a chat with the appointed judge, either over drinks the evening before, or over breakfast early the morning of the show. He shared some of the peculiarities of the horses, identifying which ones were stubborn, which were skittish, which were easy to handle, which were challenging. That way the judge could form a better idea of who was handling the horse and who was literally being taken for a ride. This was important, because at Far's shows, judging was based solely on the rider. These were equitation, not performance classes; equitation over jumps, not advanced hunter classes.

Stoney Johnston was not one to loll around during cocktail hour, so she arrived with the sun for her pre-show briefing. While she and Far sat in lumpy leather chairs in the library discussing horses, Vera and I were shunted out the back door to lend a hand in the barn. I went out somewhat reluctantly, not because I wanted to shirk my stable duties, but because I had seen the Cerilli's silver and green American Traveler pull up a few minutes earlier. Nonetheless, I pulled on my newly polished riding boots and went out to face the day…and the music.

⊣ • ⊢

Now, I expect all of you are anticipating the awkward adolescent moment that is destined to come next, since the experience of childhood crushes, or *ungdomsforelskelse* as we say in Norwegian (a pretty big word for such an everyday occurrence), must be nigh unto universal. But on this occasion it wasn't really that bad. No sooner had I opened the garden gate than Anna spotted me and came running… ok, maybe not running, but hurrying anyway…to greet me.

"Hi, Dag. How are you?"

You can imagine how my spirits soared at the profundity, the insight, the magnitude of these words.

"Can't complain," I replied with equal intelligence.

"Are you ready?"

For what? I thought briefly. For the show, of course.

"Yeah, I guess so." (Quite the conversationalist, wasn't I?)

"Well, may the best rider win," she chirped. Then, casting me one of her patented, make-you-melt smiles, she skipped away.

Oddly enough, I can't for the life of me recall what Anna's horse was named. He was a big, strapping bay gelding, the kind of animal someone had bred for three-day eventing, a year or two past his prime, but still an impressive and willing mount. Anna always did well in Pony Club trials and hunter classes. She looked tiny on top of that big horse — he must have been at least sixteen-two — but once in the saddle, she was a strong, no-nonsense rider. They made quite a pair. Viking and I were no match for them, even on our best days.

I was scheduled to ride in three classes that day; all against Anna and her gelding. We were signed up for an equitation class for ages 12-16, which I was looking forward to, and an equitation over jumps for ages

12-16, which I was dreading, even though Viking and I both fit the age category. I was also signed up to ride in the junior hunter class. This was an event Viking and I rarely attempted, and never with any great success. But a friend of Far's, a former stable hand named Bill Shorter, was bringing a second-year green hunter named Gray Smoke that he wanted to season before the summer show circuit. Bill had suggested I ride the horse in the junior class, and I accepted without giving it much thought. I had ridden Gray Smoke a few times, but only once over low fences. Nonetheless I liked him. He was a beautiful animal and a willing jumper. Besides, I was young. I was invincible. I could ride anything.

The day, as you might expect, would put that confidence to a severe test.

As 9:00 o'clock drew closer, activity around the barn and show ring grew more focused. Entrants began tacking up their mounts. Randy and Marshall double-checked to make sure all the academy horses were saddled, bridled and ready to go. Far posted courses for the jumping and hunter classes and the list of entries in each class. This was, after all, a low-key affair. Entries were accepted until the day before the show. There were no programs. Riders were identified by cardboard numbers that hung on metal hooks from the back of each rider's collar. Folks crowded around the listings to check out the competition and memorize the sequence of jumps for each jumping class.

On the far side of the ring, Farmor had set up her lawn chair in the shade of a black cherry sapling. She had her knitting basket on one side and a cooler with water and cold boiled potatoes on the other. She also had a book handy, in case the equestrian competition couldn't hold her attention.

"I like horses," she would say, "but you can't talk to a horse the way you talk to a person."

In one way she was right. On the other hand, the way you talk to a horse can sometimes beat the socks off the way you talk to people. But

Farmor was a people-person. She enjoyed four-legged critters from a distance, and mostly for their adornment value. She was a soft boot all the way.

At last, Far stepped up to the public address microphone and welcomed everyone to Twin Brook Acres for the Spring Horse Show. He then turned the proceedings over to the announcer, a favored university student, and the show was on.

The first class, equitation for ages 6-8, was always a treat. Little people with riding helmets that made their heads look gigantic, on top of horses in all shapes and sizes. Some of the youngsters didn't have legs long enough to reach below the saddle flap. But they could be a determined bunch. They kicked and hollered and used their whips and, regrettably, jerked far too often on the reins, sometimes to give a message to the horse, but just as often to keep their own balance.

During this first class, Far always stood inside the ring, and at the judge's request would call out instructions to the riders. "TROT, Everyone TROT," he would shout in his stentorian tone, occasionally even adding the "Up-Down-Up-Down" instructions for posting. "Aaaaaand, CANTER!" he commanded. "WALK. Everyone Waaaaalk," in a precise diminuendo.

To the casual observer, the little riders were surprisingly good at taking their oversized mounts through all these paces. But at the academy, we knew different. That voice inside the ring was the secret. It was the voice of the true master, the voice every single academy horse heard every day, the voice that belonged to the trainer, tutor and disciplinarian, the voice that meant food and shelter as well.

In later years I had the chance to train horses myself, to get an animal accustomed to hearing my voice and commands. It was a humbling and rewarding experience. One gentle and trusting Thoroughbred filly I worked with got so used to my voice I could turn her loose in a ring and simply shout commands. She would trot or canter in circles around me without training reins or a lounge line or whip. The same was true at the horse show. The academy horses were going to do what Far said, no matter what signals their riders gave. And horses being horses, the herd being the herd, any newcomers would follow suit.

It happened, of course, that a mount would get a notion and suddenly head off in the opposite direction. Or stop abruptly to taste that luscious red clover at ringside. Without fail, a parent would dart out of the surroundings, waving an arm or brandishing a crop to move the wayward beast back into the fold.

For judge Stoney Johnston, it was not a question of which child was actually riding the horse. It was more a question of who was using the right tools, who had the moves down, who would, given time and a little more heft, ultimately be able to communicate with the animal. In the meantime, the horses moved in sync with Far's commands. It made for an intriguing charade. Watching the little tykes struggling to get with the program delighted us older kids as much as it perplexed the nervous parents.

When the 8-through-11 class entered the ring, I brought Viking out of the barn, rubbed him down and stretched his legs the way we had seen Thoroughbred trainers do at Keeneland. I led him off to a quiet corner of the field away from the hubbub of the show ring. Before mounting, I talked gently to him and watched his ears flicker between my voice and the distant murmur of the PA system. He held his head high, his tail arched. He knew it was not a day for a casual ride in the park.

"Let's at least get a first or second in this equitation class," I suggested.

Viking cast me a doleful stare.

"OK. I ask too much. How about you just take your canter leads right off?"

The old fellow cocked his head as if to say he'd think about it.

Our competition was stiff. Anna and her horse (the one whose name I can't remember) were always a threat. Jack and Cavalier could never be counted out, although they specialized more in hunter events. One of the newer students was on Silver Jim, the Olympic Trials champion. There was Jo Dabney and her roan quarter horse, Tiki. And Coley Calloway was riding Gay Blade, that proud American Saddlebred who never once missed a canter lead. Tough crowd. Luckily, Vera had moved on to the next age level, or she, too, would have been a threat. There were years when Vera and Silver Jim were an unbeatable pair. But as I recall, this was one of my sister's last shows. She had begun to trade her boots in for the musical instruments and textbooks that would occupy the rest of her life.

I took Viking through his warm-ups away from the crowd. He began to relax a bit, to stretch out. We did several figure eights at a slow trot, and his neck began to flex from side to side. I pulled him to a walk, but kept him moving energetically. His front feet began to reach, his hooves moved more crisply. Finally, I took him through wide circles at the canter. He went into the gait easily, following the signals I sent with my hands, legs and weight.

I felt like we were ready when they called our class into the ring.

An equitation class with 10-12 riders takes about 15-20 minutes to complete. The riders are asked to go through all three gaits — walk, trot and canter — in both directions, while the judge evaluates the riders' ability to control movement and maximize the horse's agility. Horses are naturally lethargic. It takes a good rider to bring out the flashiness in them, the pride and elegance that always lies buried within.

During that equitation class, I never once looked at judge Johnston. Her assistant (another university student serving as ringmaster) barked out orders and Viking and I did our best to follow them. I was vaguely aware of the others around me, Anna's gelding moving gracefully across the ring, Jo's roan mare cantering smartly ahead of me, Jack somewhere close by being nonchalant yet fashionable Jack.

At last the class was called to one end of the ring to await Ms. Stoney's decision. The ringmaster couriered a sheet of paper to the announcer. I saw Mom hand a batch of ribbons and a thimble of a trophy to a long-time client and her daughter. They came to the center of the ring and the announcement began:

"Sixth place — Jack desCognets riding Cavalier."

"Well," I whispered to Viking, "We're either better than sixth or worse."

"Fifth place — Coley Calloway on Gay Blade."

"Whew."

"Fourth place — Lisa Cromwell on Silver Jim."

"Still a chance."

"Third place — Dag Ryen on Viking."

Well, you can't win them all. And as I rode forward to get my yellow ribbon, I knew who would follow me. "Second — Jo Dabney." And first place went to Anna Cerilli on some unnamed giant gelding.

⊣ • ⊢

What are the parameters of disappointment? What are the countless ways we humans set ourselves up to be disappointed? How can we be so stupid? Or is it really stupidity? Is there a pathological side to the problem? Can we really control these behavioral consequences. If so, how does disappointment become so intense, so visceral?

The lexicographer tells us that disappointment is "non-fulfillment of expectation or desire." That should be fair warning. Any time you begin to expect something — like winning a horse show, for instance — any time you allow desire to appear, you're setting yourself up. Psychologists will of course tell us there are rational and irrational desires. Hence, we have rational and irrational disappointment. The former can be a positive developmental tool, an experience that promotes greater self-awareness, greater commitment and ultimately greater personal strength. The latter is a dark hole, offering no such benefit, no behavioral consolation prize. The trick is knowing the difference.

I went into lunch that day decidedly glum, in hindsight clearly suffering from irrational disappointment. I didn't realize that for the first time in our competitive career, Viking and I had beat the two academy stars, Silver Jim and Gay Blade. The one thing that stuck in my addled adolescent mind was that I hadn't distinguished myself sufficiently. I hadn't done enough to attract attention. Such are the senseless expectations that bring us down.

Farmor, perhaps on a quest to raid the fridge for more cold potatoes, found me sitting at the kitchen table. I must have looked the part of the sadsack, because she immediately sat down across from me.

"*Er det noe i veien?*" she asked.

I offer this sentence in Norwegian, because the translator has two choices: "Is there something in the road?" or "Is something wrong?" Of course she meant the latter, but the applicability of the former is what struck me. There were some serious bumps in the road ahead.

In my flustered way, I tried to explain to Farmor. "No. I...just thought we did really well...I guess...I thought we had a chance to win."

I expected the standard response, the "winning isn't everything — you should be happy you did well."

But Farmor did me one better. "It's not for you to judge how well you did...or whether you won, or whether you should have won. Others might decide for now, but ultimately, only God can decide."

It was the kind of kitchen table mini-sermon of which Farmor seemed to have an endless supply. And while I've never gotten completely comfortable with how God fits into this process, I've learned to respect her advice about letting others decide. I still don't always follow it. But it is good advice.

Farmor went on. "When you fall off the horse, you have to get right back on."

Now she was back on familiar turf. These were words I'd heard in a thousand different contexts, a dozen different phrasings.

"You're never a good rider until you lose count of how many times you've fallen off."

"Out of the saddle and onto the ground; back in the saddle to turn things around."

"The only way to improve is to conquer the beast that threw you."

"Hitting the dirt give you a fright? Back up again will make it all right."

These were the aphorisms that carried me through childhood and right into adolescence. These saws, along with the occasional comments of a wizened Norwegian country wife, bore me into adulthood with a reasonable helping of good sense and better than average curiosity. Without them, I would have dared so little.

⊣ • ⊢

I did hit the dirt that afternoon, hit it hard. Coming up on the third jump in the equitation over fences class, Viking had one of his optical illusions. I felt his body quiver under me at a full canter. "Look," it said, "there's a giant, fire-breathing dragon hiding under that chicken coop." Viking's ears snapped forward, his neck arched like a spent bowstring. His front hooves stiffened and dug miniature canyons in the soft ground as we shuddered to an abrupt halt.

But I didn't fall off. Not yet.

I settled deep into the saddle, murmured some soothing words to my mount, gently guided him around in a large circle, began encouraging him with a series of c'mon boy, you-can-do-its and straightened up for another run at the fence. This time, the intrepid horse charged straight toward the chicken coop, and this time there was no hesitation. I checked him, gauged his pace and released him two strides from the jump. Up we went. Up and over.

It was there, in mid-air, that Viking and I encountered the giant, fire-breathing dragon. It was, in fact, a tiny cottontail rabbit cowering behind the chicken coop. Seeing this humongous six-legged shadow descending on it from the sky, the little rabbit darted first one way, then the other. Viking, exhibiting an almost palpable fear of harming the tiny creature began to twist and contort in all directions. Somewhere between this direction and that we parted company. I went sailing over his head, did a somersault, and hit the ground helmet first. Luckily, I had the presence of mind to roll as I came down. As I wheeled to one side, I saw Viking still going through incredible contortions to avoid coming down either on top of me or the poor little bunny rabbit, who still hadn't abandoned this treacherous equine arena for safer burrows. In an unlikely display of agility, Viking stuck out one front leg and one back leg to catch his weight, and tucked the other two under him, the two that would have struck me or the rabbit hard. Then Viking, too, rolled away from the potential carnage.

And while I can't recall the name of Anna's gelding, I will never, as long as I live, forget what lengths that crazy old wonderful horse of mine went to to avoid injuring either me, his tormentor and sometime friend, or that napped bunny. When we struggled to our feet moments later, both somewhat dazed, he came to me and I went to him, as if asking, "What happened? Are you all right?"

The answer was fortunately, yes. "Back in the saddle to turn things around." I remounted. And, as if nothing had happened, we were once more on our way, over another dozen fences without a hitch, maybe a turn too choppy or a departure too abrupt, but no hesitation and no miscommunication. When we finished, I dropped the reins, wrapped my arms around his course neck and gave Viking a giant-sized hug.

At that point, it didn't matter what the announcer said. After a fall, the chances of a ribbon were practically nil. Half the kids had ridden a clean course. Anna and Jack had both done wonderfully. Coley, Jo, Lisa, Rab had all done better than me.

Not so, decreed judge Stoney Johnston.

"Third place — Dag Ryen on Viking."

I rode mystified into the center of the ring to pick up my yellow ribbon. The grim hardboot herself broke protocol and walked over to us. "Nice job," judge Johnston said. "No one could have stayed on through that spill. And you were riding him every inch of the way, both before and after. Nice job."

As I said before, shows at the riding academy were judged on the rider, not the horse. Yet I hold out that yellow ribbon as the most well deserved prize Viking ever won.

⊣ • ⊢

No one fussed over me after the class. Of course Mom was on me the minute we cleared the course to make sure I hadn't hurt myself. Even Far cast a questioning eye in my direction and then turned his attention back to running the show. And Anna did say "Congratulations!" as she rode by with her second blue ribbon. Jack came over and asked to borrow a hoof pick. Rab asked if I had lost any marbles.

None of that really mattered.

When I hopped aboard Gray Smoke a short time later to warm up for the cross-country class, the tiny waves of dizziness had left my head but the adrenaline was still coursing. Right away, I connected with the elegant gray. I held his mouth gently in my reins. I felt his body flex with every squeeze of my legs. I sensed his concentration.

Our turn came to tackle the course, and for the next several minutes, Gray Smoke and I shared that wonderful feeling of perfect teamwork. He was a performer as well as an athlete. He flew over the fences with panache and enjoyed every challenge. He let me pace him and responded to my every suggestion. Heading into the logs, I checked him to avoid a rough spot. At the creek crossing, I steadied him just when a hind leg began to slip on wet rock. Over the brush, we literally flew, twice as high and twice as far as we needed, simply because it was fun and easy and wonderful.

When we were done, I became faintly aware of a ripple of applause from the spectators. But again it didn't matter. There would be plenty of time for judging when all life's bumps were behind us, as Farmor would say.

However, when you least need it and least expect it, attention often rains down. Even as the last two competitors negotiated the course, family and friends descended on me from all sides. I was standing by the barn with a horse in each hand. Jack gave me a toothsome smile and handshake. Vera crowed, "Way to go, bro." Anna stood beside me and seemed to echo everyone's praise with her lilting laughter. Farmor shuffled up and gave me a mountain-sized hug that made the whole crowd crack up.

And out of nowhere, Melissa Turner appeared. She came over to us and my little coterie seemed to part as if to give way to her royal entourage. Somewhere in the background I noticed Randy, also beaming. His queen looked stunning, as always. She cocked her head slightly, reached out to shake my hand, and said, "You know, you're a very good rider."

For once I knew what to say. "No. I had a very good horse." In fact, that day I had two darn good horses.

Then, all too soon, I had to break away from my fans to retrieve my tiny trophy and blue ribbon. Even Stoney Johnston permitted a smile to cross her somber lips as I trotted into the ring with a proud Gray Smoke on one side and the humble Viking on the other.

Looking back over a long and eventful life, I find there are precious few moments I would want to relive. But this was definitely one…in all its self-adulatory glory. I could have stood there for weeks, surrounded by friends and admirers, basking not only in my own glory, but in a new-found piece of understanding. On that sunny May day I had learned a few critical things about myself, a few useful things about others, and one truly amazing thing about horses. If you talk to them right, they do whatever they can for you. They may not always be up to it, but they try. That, too, is advice I've always sought to follow. At the very least, you can give it a try.

CHAPTER VII

ALWAYS BE THINKING
ABOUT THE NEXT FENCE

And so I entered the summer of '59 armed with a new-found sense of discovery. My senses were activated; my antennae extended. And I was headed straight into that astonishing mix of surprise, pain and joy that makes life such a trip.

As soon as school was out, we settled into our customary summer routine, spending long afternoons grooming and hacking, lounging, lolling, and pestering Randy. We would ride, work, play and relax as Far negotiated his afternoon classes. We would patrol the barn and environs with abandon, then, as the sun settled in the West, we would gather in the little stable office and debrief the highlights and non-events, most of which suggested permanence, only a few of which signaled change.

Had I been less cloistered, I might have had a sharper sense of impending change. I might have been more aware of the emergence of new obstacles. I might have heeded Far's constant counsel to always be thinking about the next fence. Before your horse lands, he would say, you must have in mind where you're going, what the next jump looks like. Had I listened, I might have seen things coming more clearly. But I didn't. Instead, I languished in blissful ignorance in the stable office.

I remember an old wooden chair in that little room. It was painted gray, as were the desk and two padlocked lockers. It was one of those so-called captain's chairs that had the contours of a human *bakparti* (derriere, butt, rump — take your pick) carved out of the seat. I remember marveling at how big adults were expected to be, and I remember measuring my own growth from summer to summer by how much I filled that old gray chair.

The lockers were another source of mystery. One was for the stable hands. They could keep personal items, a change of shoes or boots, or rain gear. Some of the lads kept a radio, although Far was very particular about what kind of music emanated from those boxes, especially when there were customers around. The other was the stable "safe," where the cash box got stowed together with various items of moderate value: special medicines, a battery-amplified megaphone and the Winchester over-and-under that Far kept around for vermin. It was always a sign that the lads had passed their probationary employment period when Far told them how to open that locker. I can't remember when he shared the combination with me, but I always knew it.

The days quickly became an indistinct blur. As temperature and humidity climbed, we spent more and more time seeking shade. We would ride back to the farthest reaches of Blue Grass Park, past the end of the airport runway to South Elkhorn Creek, where a few old growth trees reached far into the sky and their thick canopies filtered out all but the gentlest rays. There we would dismount, secure the horses by flipping reins around a low branch (something Far never would have approved of), and settle up against a century-old bole to watch the haze and listen to incisors nibbling buffalo clover.

There was one blue ash in particular, at the edge of the woods on a slight rise above the bottom land. That spot afforded a soothing view of creek and foliage, with the gently sloping fields of Stoney Point Farm in the background. It was our favorite spot. If the sun hit just right, we could make out the ripples as the current played around the old millstone John Parker had used at one of several grist mills he ran along the South Elkhorn in the early 1800s.

There were other things to watch back in this section of the park. All kinds of critters, for instance. Weasels, mink, red and gray foxes, muskrats and a multitude of red squirrels. Also, the YMCA ran a day camp for kids along the banks of the creek. There were ball fields, an archery range and a large pavilion for picnics. Camp organizers pitched a series of tepees around the pavilion. Each batch of campers would divide into tribes, and camp activities would take the form of contests between Apache and Navajo, Utes and Cherokee, Shawnee and Blackfoot.

From our vantage point on the rise, we could follow the goings-on without being disturbed. We could sit and discuss weighty matters without fear of being interrupted or overheard. Or, at least we could until disaster struck.

One Friday afternoon in early June, we arrived to find our hallowed resting place violated. In preparing for summer sessions, the YMCA had encroached on our sanctuary. The archery range had spilled out of the valley and crept up the hill. There was a giant straw bullseye right next to the trunk of our blue ash, right where an errant arrow might endanger both resting rider and grazing beast.

Needless to say, we didn't much care for the intrusion. We fumed about it for weeks.

We had no legal claim, no special usage rights in the park, except that we used it more than anyone else...a lot more than anyone else. The public came for picnics during the summer, or for an occasional soap box derby or family reunions at the pavilion. But mostly during the summer. From September to May, we had the run of the place. In the carefree tranquility that was the late 1950s, my friends and I — you know who you are — traversed these fields and woods year round. After a snowfall, we created patterns in the snow, large wheels with spokes where we played mounted tag. Far arranged Easter egg hunts in April and scavenger hunts in October, tying red pipe cleaners around branches throughout the park's hundreds of acres. Whoever found the most markers won a prize, a candy bar, free soda or sometimes, a new riding crop that Barkley's or Meyer's had sent over as thanks for our business.

Little wonder, then, that we took a dim view of the YMCA's incursion. We had dibs on that blue ash, odal rights. We were the first-born and first arrived. We were the indigenous ones, the keepers of the South Elkhorn spirit. Little wonder we began to harbor resentment for the brazen archers who claimed our birthright. So, licking our wounds, we retreated into the woods and began to ponder some form of retribution.

I've mentioned a couple of times how schools can misguide us, how book learning only scratches the surface of knowledge. The matter of indigenous American Indians is a case in point. I'm certain the YMCA day campers picked up lots of pointers on how to make fancy headdresses out of blue jay and red-tailed hawk feathers, or how to fold a tepee flap to keep rain out. And I'm equally certain they didn't learn diddly about the real Indians who set foot in the Bluegrass long before white settlers made the trek across Cumberland Gap.

For one, the Shawnee and Cherokee who used central Kentucky as hunting grounds didn't have tepees. Their homes in Ohio and Tennessee were log houses or lean-tos, permanent abodes erected close to arable fields where the women cultivated corn, beans and squash. Among the Southeastern Indians, including the Cherokee, the women owned the buildings and determined how the fields were to be planted. An Indian town could encompass dozens of families and up to a hundred dwellings.

The men traveled in small groups to harvest deer, elk and an occasional bison from the Bluegrass. A handful of arrowheads and skinning tools collected along the creeks at Twin Brook Acres attest to their presence. Sometimes, disputes would erupt between rival hunting parties. Sometimes, blood would be shed. But the image of face-painted warriors donning fancy headdresses to go on the warpath is a figment of Hollywood's and the YMCA's imagination. The Cherokee and Shawnee used feathers and deerskin for all kinds of clothing and domestic articles. Headdresses were for ritual use, for the ceremonies held to ensure a good harvest or the health of the clan. There is no reliable evidence that Kentucky was ever a "dark and bloody ground" where savages battled over rights to the land.

The truth is that land ownership was, and remains, foreign to most native American cultures. The Indians who harassed settlers in Kentucky were incensed because whites had the gall to believe they could own land outright, to the exclusion of anyone else. Early settlers never understood the native concept that land was a common asset of all peoples, that fruits of the land were gifts from the spirits, not chattel to be amassed. Indian attacks increased in the 1770s and 1780s not because native Americans felt territorially threatened, but because French and British agents paid them in guns, bullets and whiskey to do the bidding of European kings. This is the manner by which we taught the uncivilized savages how to behave.

I suppose my mounted friends and I, as well as the YMCA day campers, would have profited greatly from a better understanding of native American cosmology. Then we might have understood that privacy is not tied to property nor majesty to wealth nor dignity to conquest. Then we might have understood that the land owns itself, that we humans are merely stewards, short-term guests with certain privileges and precious few rights.

But I digress...

⊢ • ⊣

Unless there was a horse show going on somewhere, Saturdays were set aside for Far's mounted troop. Seven or eight of the guys would get together to practice the close order drills we did publicly, patterned after the tattoos of the Royal Canadian Mounted Police, or worked on our lance skills by spearing doughnuts strung overhead with baling twine. We had two "real" lances that we used for performances, and a bunch of very serviceable bamboo poles. When the serious work was over and Far had been called away to other duties or other clients, many of the troopers lingered. We would go for trail rides in the park or play polo in the outdoor ring, "sticking around" as it was appropriately called. This was Viking's favorite time of the week, a time for play with no competitive pressure. In a way, I agreed with him. It was mighty nice being a kid at heart, with no demands or responsibilities. Few kids and not a whole lot of horses get to enjoy that part of life.

Another great activity, one we only got to do a couple of times a year, was twilight capture-the-flag. If conditions were right — the temperature not too hot and not too cold, the ground not too hard and not too soft, the number of picnickers not too daunting — we would divide up into teams, rig up a big red flag and a big green flag, and head off into the fading twilight.

We had the entire park divided into zones; a red zone, a green zone and a buffer zone. Red team would ride to the far reaches of the park, back by the YMCA camp, while green team would hold close to the quarry and picnic grounds. Each team would establish a sanctuary, a place where the flag was kept and prisoners held. The sanctuary had to be a circle at least fifty feet in diameter and no defensive player was allowed inside.

Mounted troop inspection

The broad fields in between were no-man's land. I remember a map we kept posted in the tack room for a while, delineating where no-man's land began and ended and noting several spots that made good sanctuaries.

The object of the game was simply to ride in and capture the other team's flag, then carry it across no-man's land into your own territory without getting caught. Whoever managed to get both flags into their sanctuary won. When Far first taught us the game, he tied long crepe streamers to each rider's waist. If a member of the opposing team got close enough to tear off a piece of your streamer, you were considered "captured" — like the familiar game of tag — and had to follow your captor back to his sanctuary. If you captured a raider carrying your flag, he, too, had to follow you back to sanctuary.

As we grew older, we grew bolder. The crepe streamers disappeared and "capturing" evolved into the simpler, and sometimes easier act of touching an opposing player. Getting the horse wasn't enough; you had to touch the rider himself. Toward the end, we got really daring and played the game with lances and swords. To our credit, we had enough sense to stick corks on the sharper weapons. Amazingly, no one ever got seriously hurt during these adrenalin-pumped evening duels. Spills were not uncommon as riders went through unbelievable contortions to avoid being touched, and a bruise or two was par for the course. But no one ever complained, and though Far sometimes wondered aloud why the bamboo lances disappeared when we went on evening trail rides, he never pressed the point.

There was one time that June, just as the stars were sprinkling across the warm evening sky, that Viking and I worked our way around the back of the red zone sanctuary by wading stealthily up South Elkhorn Creek. There was a good bit of water and the splashing current covered our sound. We climbed quietly up the bank and, keeping the YMCA pavilion between us and the Red Team rider — Coley, if memory serves — who was patrolling the sanctuary, we inched through the woods toward our goal. When we were no more than 100 feet away, we stopped and waited for our adversary to give us an opening.

Viking loved the game. He stood still as a heron on a mudflat, ears perked, nostrils flared, ready for my signal. Somewhere off in the distance, a twig snapped. Coley gave his horse a slight nudge and headed off to inspect. That was the chance we needed. My charger and I broke out of the woods, darted into the red sanctuary, and snatched up the flag. I tucked it under my arm together with my bamboo lance and charged into the open fields at a full gallop with Coley in hot pursuit.

Strangely, what I remember from that awesome, riotous ride was laughter. As Viking's hooves pounded the ground beneath me and as Coley's full lung shouts summoned his teammates behind, and as the great velvet blue "*hvelving*" of the evening sky seemed to envelop me, I was laughing my head off. It wasn't funny. It wasn't panic. It was the laughter of joy, the laughter of having one hell of a wonderful time out there in the night with few cares and little sense and a handful of good friends with which to waste the fading days of childhood.

Needless to say, we made it. With all three Red Team riders converging on us from three sides, Viking and I ducked through a tight knot of trees, cut across the picnic area, jumped a park bench when one of the Reds got too close and dashed into Green sanctuary only yards ahead of the nearest pursuer.

It was exhilarating. It was textbook.

I believe that may have been the very last time I permitted myself the uninhibited laughter of innocence.

⊣ • ⊢

Don't get me wrong. Innocence isn't all it's cracked up to be. There are real benefits to growing up. It's just too bad the other stuff comes with it.

My innocence began to unravel the following Sunday. (For the more squeamish among you, let me hasten to say that I will be talking about emotional innocence, not the x-rated kind. You can get plenty of that from prime time television or a good Norwegian movie.) It began to unravel when I discovered new feelings that I couldn't control and didn't appreciate and wished would go away.

We were at the Polo Club, a portion of Hamburg Place that had been turned into a sort of private club for the equine set. It wasn't fancy. There was no big mansion like the Lexington Country Club, no understated elegance like Idle Hour. It was mostly a patio, dressing rooms for men and women, and a delightfully unique swimming pool.

The pool at the Polo Club was made out of cut limestone block, like the stone fences of the Bluegrass. It was fed by cold, crystal clear water from a nearby spring, and the maintenance crew never adulterated it with a drop of chlorine. A few crystals of copper sulfate, "bluestone," kept the algae and insects at bay. But frogs loved that pool. And the occasional minnow or darter made its way through the feeder line. A time or two, we even had to eject a garter snake who had gone in for an afternoon dip. Biologically speaking, it was an equal opportunity pool.

The Polo Club pool was the perfect antidote for hot summer doldrums. When the air got so heavy you needed a machete to cut through it and the humidity squeezed past saturation, it was the only place to be.

Jack's nanny would often drive us out on Sunday afternoons. We would refresh ourselves in the nippy waters, maybe play a game or two

The Polo Club at Hamburg Place

of Marco Polo, dangle our feet over the edge while talking about nothing in particular, then head home for supper with our families.

But on this particular Sunday, when we arrived it seemed as if everyone we knew was there. Several of the kids we rode in horse shows with, or hunted with, or were in the Pony Club with, were already frolicking poolside. To my chagrin, I quickly spotted Anna Cerilli among them.

I shouldn't trouble you with descriptions of my thoughts when I first saw the object of my adolescent desire in her snug, white bathing suit. In fact, I won't. But something lodged securely in my throat, and my ability to say anything comprehensible for the rest of the afternoon was squelched. I managed a modest greeting, then struggled in vain to get close enough to say something vaguely coherent, all the while wondering what in the world I could possibly say.

The other memorable thing about that Sunday was unusual activity across the way at Hamburg Place. MGM had taken over one of the barns to shoot scenes for the movie, "April Love," and no lesser notables than Pat Boone and Shirley Jones were in town for the filming. Naturally, after an hour around the pool, the gang decided to head over and see what was going on.

I suspect that by today's standards, this film set would have looked definitely B-grade. There were a few microphones and lights and a couple of bulky, black cameras that looked like giant alien insects. There was a trailer off to one side that served as a combination office and green room. But most of the preparation, from make-up to final costume fitting to sound checks was all done alfresco. The director walked around with a giant megaphone, shouting instructions this way and that while a dozen technicians scurried about adjusting props and lighting.

At first we hung back, watching the proceedings from a distance, a dozen or so star-struck kids...with no stars in sight. Then, to our delight, an assistant director came over to ask if we wanted to see the set at close hand. The girls squealed with joy, the guys nodded with affected nonchalance, and we were escorted to a place of honor near the main camera. We settled down in the grass to watch. I managed to slip casually into a spot right next to Anna, and for a brief moment the day was looking up.

Filming began. The director ordered a wide pan of the surroundings, letting the lens drink in green pastures, black fences, horses grazing in the distance, spired barns and stone outbuildings. After this first shot, he motioned to an assistant who darted to the trailer and knocked energetically on the door. I'm not ashamed to admit even I emitted a small gasp when they actually emerged from the trailer, Pat Boone and Shirley Jones in person.

They stopped briefly at the make-up table, were patted with a little more powder to keep the incessant humidity in check. A couple of crew members began tugging and plucking at Ms. Jones' outfit, which seemed perfectly all right to me, if a little formal for an ordinary Bluegrass after-noon. While the adjustments were being made, the assistant director grabbed Pat Boone's arm and guided him over to where we were seated. The assistant made some vague introduction about "some kids from the neighborhood," and before we knew it we were making awkward responses to Pat Boone's questions.

"Nice to see you here. Are you enjoying yourselves?" Mr. Boone asked.

General squeals and grunts of approval.

"Ever seen a movie made before?"

Much shaking of heads.

"Well, hope you'll go see this one when it comes out," the star encouraged.

Then he moved forward, almost stepping on my outstretched bare foot, and reached toward Anna.

She jumped to her feet, beaming that patented smile.

"Hi," he smiled back, shaking her hand. "I'm Pat Boone."

Her composure didn't falter a second. "I'm Anna Cerilli, Mr. Boone, and I'm one of your biggest fans," she gushed.

"Well, thank you. I'll make sure you get an autographed photo." And without further ado, he turned, rejoined the crew and got back to the admittedly tedious business of making a motion picture.

Jealousy rears its ugly head at the most unexpected moments. Just when you think you've achieved a modicum of control over your environs, your destiny, your trembling hands and quavering larynx. Just when it almost seems as if something is within reach. That's when the green monster appears, the emotional obstacle of obstacles. Right on cue. Lights, camera, action.

Anna was in seventh heaven the rest of the afternoon. "Did you see that!?" she asked anyone and everyone. "He shook my hand," she gleefully exclaimed while extending the honored extremity.

What could a poor, tongue-tied 15-year-old offer. How could an unschooled adolescent compete with Pat Boone's honeyed voice, that famed visage, that *fløtefjes* (cream face), as the more cynical Norseman might say. No contest.

At the time I was devastated, at least as devastated as a kid my age could be. I sulked around the pool for another hour and was relieved when Jack's nanny finally came to pick us up. I even went out of my way to make sure Anna wouldn't see us leave. That'll serve her right, I figured, with classic infantile stupidity.

It was a low point. Still is, in some subtle way. I can never get over the sense of discomfort thinking how dense I was, how silly my reaction was. I had been caught off guard. I hadn't seen that fence coming.

At the same time, I still derive a tiny bit of consolation from one small fact: Pat Boone never did send Anna any autographed photo.

CHAPTER VIII

KEEP "RED" ON RIGHT

Human behavior is a splendid and mysterious thing. We go through life attaching ourselves to each other in numerous ways, building layers of loyalty, patterns of identity. Through birth, exposure, training or choice, we become associated with special groupings of like-minded individuals. As the result of continued contact with this group, we arrive at common codes of conduct covering everything from potentially destructive acts to the tiniest minutiae of social discourse. We learn not to steal and we learn to hold our forks in our right hand. We learn to say "Ma'am" and "Sir," and to stop at octagonal red signs. On the cross country course, we learn to honor "red on right," and in the hunt field we learn to stay behind the field master.

We are Citation fans or Whirlaway fans, Tiger fans, Red Sox fans or Wildcat fans. We are Lexingtonians, Kentuckians, Americans, city dwellers, farmers, students, vegetarians or veterinarians. We are mothers, fathers, sons, daughters, Jews, Christians or atheists; employees, leaders, soldiers, pacifists or Luddites; Democrats, Republicans, Socialists or Rhode Islanders. And though identity is largely fluid...we become older if slower, wiser if less passionate, more patient if more set in our ways...some elements of our identity remain intact. For many individuals, one level, one aspect of identity becomes paramount. It becomes the most important identifying characteristic.

In the political world, this is the origin of progress. We adopt causes with a passion that overrides any other consideration. We identify with issues, become obsessed with outcomes. We shed our birthright, ethnicity or education to become single-minded reformers or campaigning radicals or fearless defenders. And political change takes place when sufficient numbers of people share such an overriding passion.

⊣ • ⊢

In Bluegrass country, however, there are few reformers or radicals. There is another option. Change is not so welcome, passion not so acceptable. The hardboot exacts a special kind of commitment, upholds a different code of conduct. The hardboot assumes an identity unto himself.

This is not to say that all hardboots are alike. The horse world of the Bluegrass is a diverse environment. There are in fact many horse worlds. There is the Pony Club set and the three-day eventing set and the five-gaited set and the fox-hunting set. There is the Thoroughbred set, which itself is divided into the breeding subset and the racing subset. There are trail riders and railbirds, touts and toffs, scions and dreamers. There are drivers and chasers, trotters and pacers, riders and passengers, jocks and jokes.

Still, the different subsets of the horse world of my adolescence didn't exist in complete isolation from one another. Avid fox hunters went on to breed Thoroughbreds. Energetic pony-clubbers became driving enthusiasts. An old tobacco farmer on Parker's Mill Road bred mules as well as race horses. Down the road a piece lived a girl who rode gaited horses at the Junior League and dressage at Pony Club rallies. All thrived within an hour's drive of Elkhorn Creek, within view of the gently rolling fields of the central Kentucky plateau, within reach of the proverbial brass ring.

One of the important bridges in this diverse horse world was our regular veterinarian, the inestimable Dr. Robert Hensley, whose no-nonsense approach to horse-doctoring and willingness to minimize vet bills quickly cemented Far's loyalty. Dr. Hensley had grown up in the saddlebred world, but built a broad and thriving practice in central Kentucky that included everything from Shetlands to Trakhaners. Whether Colpin became cholicy, a yearling colt needed a poultice or a broodmare needed palping, Bob Hensley was our man for the job. But true to his gaited horse roots, he always seemed to bear a special fondness for Gay Blade, the academy's saddlebred beauty.

In my own life, there was a significant overlap between the hunter-jumper environment and the Thoroughbred world. As soon as we moved to the farm in the late 1950s, Far picked up a couple of cheap broodmares and began producing yearlings for the Keeneland and Fasig-Tipton auctions. Occasionally, a colt wouldn't fetch the reserve and he'd return to the farm for breaking and training.

I can't say Far was ever wildly successful with the horses he took to the track. But I know he got a big kick out of it. Mornings when he loaded He's Off to head for River Downs or Latonia were among his happiest. He was always smiling as he bolted the trailer gate, always optimistic. It was anticipation that generated this joy, the perhaps irrational hope that today might be the day when the colt puts it all together, when a two-minute sustained effort leads to the winner's circle and a heap of rewards...of which rekindled hope was possibly the most important.

"This-could-be-the-day." That's the spirit that drives horsemen and horsewomen all over the world. It's an infectious spirit, an ailment that is mighty hard to get rid of once it gets into you.

⊣ • ⊢

My father summoned me into his office one morning a few weeks after school was out. This was not entirely uncommon, though it usually signified something momentous, at least by adolescent standards. He motioned me into a chair across from the big wooden desk where he devised grand strategies for clients, the menagerie and himself. I settled back, wondering which chin strap I had left unsoaped or which water bucket insufficiently scoured. But Far seemed to be in a good mood. He eyed me with that narrowed, twinkling gaze which always seemed to convey a hint of mischief.

He ran a hand across his glistening hairless dome and began, "There are a couple of things I wanted to talk to you about."

"Yes, sir." (I always spoke respectfully to my father, though in a way that displayed more affection than fear.)

"First, I want to talk to you about the Pony Club rally."

My heart sank. This was not a subject I was keen to discuss. Ever since the disastrous afternoon at the Polo Club, I'd been avoiding any thought of rallies or teams or competitive activities of any kind.

"Yes, sir," I responded half-heartedly.

"Well, I know you've been concerned about how Viking would do in the team trials. He's a good horse in many ways, but there hasn't been much time to make an event horse out of him, has there?"

He paused, waiting for some response from me.

"No, sir. He's a good horse, but pretty green over fences."

My father nodded. "That's what I was thinking. So I had a talk with Bill Shorter. I suggested that maybe we could lease Gray Smoke for a couple of months, just long enough for you to ride him in the tryouts, and then in the rally if you make the team. Bill's so busy he's not getting the horse enough work."

I'm sure my jaw dropped to where my heart had been.

"Would you like that?" Far asked, seeking confirmation of the obvious.

"Would I? Yes, sir!"

"Good. I'll make the arrangements. Of course, this means you'll have to take full responsibility for the horse while we have him. Regular exercise, grooming every day, and so on..." Another pause.

"Absolutely. I'll take extra good care of him."

"Good. Then there's another thing."

I swallowed, wondering what earth-shattering news was next.

"As part of this arrangement, I think it would be appropriate for you to help cover the expenses. You know, another horse means more feed and more bedding and more overhead."

"I know, sir," I said, seeing my $5 a month allowance go up in smoke, gray smoke at that. So much for a certain movie date I had been harboring secret dreams about.

"Well, as it turns out," Far went on, "they could use some extra help out at Clovelly. They have five horses going in the summer sales and Lars is a little short-handed. He'll pay you $2.50 an hour. You can keep half and the other half will go to upkeep for the horse."

I was puzzled. "You mean prepping sales yearlings." I had visions of a feisty, strapping colt batting me around the stall like a beach ball.

"Yes. I think you're ready for it."

"But how would I get out there and back. And how would I find time for my chores around here?" I saw my whole waking life being buried under piles of stained yellow straw.

As usual, Far had the whole thing worked out. "It's really only a little more than two weeks until the sales horses ship to Keeneland," he explained. "Until then, we'll drive you out there and you can stay with the LaCours. Randy and Marshall can take care of things here. Once the sales start, it will be easy. You could even walk to Keeneland. Then, when it's over, we'll bring Gray Smoke in and you can resume your chores. How does that sound?"

I was overwhelmed. But the plan sounded exciting...exciting and a little bit scary. I'd groomed a lot of horses, but not too many high-strung, full-blooded yearlings. On the other hand, any horse raised by Lars LaCour was raised to be well behaved. Maybe I could handle it. Maybe it was time to move past the pat answers of AG 132 and find out if I really did understand animal husbandry.

"I guess it sounds fine," I replied, "if you think I can do it."

"Oh, you won't have any trouble," Far reassured me. "You've been around horses all your life."

My father had that way of making everything sound so simple. That was part of what made him such a good teacher. He instilled confidence by being confident himself. He conveyed understanding of the subject by bringing the subject literally into your life. He supplemented knowledge with experience and then let time turn knowledge into wisdom. His pedagogical paradigm was flawless. And when he said I could do it, I instinctively believed him. After all, I had been around horses all my life. But more importantly, I had been around my father all my life. What more could I need?

When I think back on that conversation, I can see Far's face clearly in front of me, the horizontal eyes, the thin lips, the active brow, the large-ish but masculine ears. All my life, people have told me how much I resemble my father. And it's true that when I look at pictures of us, I can see the resemblance. My eyes are narrow, my hairline now receding, my brow furrowed. But when I think of Far today, I have a wonderful sense of how different we are, and an even more cherished sense of how important those differences were to both of us.

We would always follow the hardboot rules, but in a world surrounded by hardboots, we would each have secret dreams to follow. Because we were that much alike, we understood each other. Because we were that much different, we enjoyed each other's company. It was a nice balance.

⊣ • ⊢

That afternoon at the barn, I got confirmation of how Far affected other people's lives as well. "Your father is a rare man: a great boss and a friend at the same time," Randy beamed. He was even more animated than usual.

We were in the stable office, tidying up, stowing supplies in lockers and drawers. I could see no apparent reason for this unsolicited testimonial. "What's going on?" I asked suspiciously.

"Nothing special. He's just letting me go early today."

"Must be something. Far never lets anyone go early without good reason."

Randy flashed a sphinx-like smile. "Like I said, your father is an understanding man." He stowed his work boots into the locker and slipped on a pair of polished penny loafers. Reaching for a comb from his back pocket, he inadvertently dislodged his wallet. It crashed to the floor, sending driver's license, photos and a small foil package marked "Trojans" skittering across the floor.

Randy looked at me briefly before retrieving his belongings. To his credit he neither winked nor blushed. His smile remained constant, the bright visage of hope, an inclusive look. It said without words that he hoped I, too, would be understanding.

I suppose I was. It surely didn't surprise me when, a quarter hour later Melissa's gold Mercedes purred up the drive. A quick hug, a peck on the cheek and seconds later they were gone, with Randy at the wheel and she contentedly curled in the passenger seat, her golden hair loose to the wind as they rode away.

I remember gulping.

⊣ • ⊢

The following Monday, I stumbled out of bed an hour before sun-up, grabbed a suitcase full of work clothes, and piled into Far's silvery Chevrolet station wagon for a long, mostly silent ride out to Paris Pike and Clovelly Farms. He dropped me off at the yearling barn with a quick "See you on Friday" and headed off. I was still sleepy, still overwhelmed, and standing in the heavy dew reminded me I was literally wet behind the ears. By the time Lars came walking up from the house, Far's Chevy was already on the main road.

I've spoken of Lars LaCour earlier, of the gentle Dane whose knowledge of horseflesh and equine behavior is legendary. He greeted me with a smile and a handshake, told me to stow the suitcase in the office for the time being and said, "Let's get to work."

I was given two yearlings to groom, a smallish bay filly by Princequillo out of a Tom Fool mare, and a gorgeous colt from Swap's second crop of yearlings. In accordance with custom, these Thoroughbreds weren't named yet, that right being reserved for the people who would buy and ultimately race them. But every yearling has a barn name. My two were "Princess" and "Bullhead." The former was as sweet as the latter was obstreperous. Princess welcomed visitors to her stall with a lowered head and a desire to be caressed. Bullhead viewed any visitor as a potential playmate and assumed that grooms were as strong and carefree and playful as he was. In short, he was a handful.

But Far was right. And I was right about Lars. Although full of energy, Bullhead was reasonably well behaved. He wasn't a nipper (maybe you didn't know that word we use affectionately for human tots comes from young horses and their instinctive habit of nipping at anything and every-thing within biting distance) and he didn't rear. On the few occasions when he actually came up off his fronts, he never struck at anything. He pulled and tugged a lot, and didn't care much for standing still. He was just a big baby having fun in a comfortable world where two-legged beings attended to his every need. He was spoiled, but good-hearted. And in time, he let me pick his hooves without making a marathon wrestling match of it.

Like many well bred race horses, Bullhead had a sense of his aristocratic roots. After all, his Daddy had won the Kentucky Derby. His Daddy had shattered world records. His Daddy had won half a million dollars on the track at a time when that was real money.

Most Kentucky hardboots hadn't cared much for Swaps, who came out of the Ellsworth stable in California. But in the 1955 Kentucky Derby, when every Bluegrass dollar was riding on the great horse Nashua or the game contender Summer Tan, Swaps came out of the pack to give them a sound licking.

Swaps and Nashua met once more, in a legendary match race at Washington Park. In the rematch, Nashua took a short lead early. Swaps closed several times along the backstretch. But each time, Nashua held the California challenger at bay, and each time Nashua's jockey, Eddie Arcaro, hounded his mount with the whip to keep the horse's mind on business. Midway through the stretch, the race was over. Swaps had given it his all and came up short. The next day, Swaps' owners announced he had aggravated an old hoof injury in the race. The brilliant chestnut would race no more that year. And there's many a railbird who claims he never was much of a race horse after that.

The Swaps-Nashua match race stands as classic testament to the competitive fire that burns in some horses. A horse like Swaps will run until he breaks. Nashua, too. Their duel has spawned a spirited discussion among enthusiasts that has spanned generations. Is it fair to pit two such high-strung competitors against each other in single combat? Is it asking for trouble? Can you run a match race without guaranteeing physical or psychological injury to the loser?

Iroquois Point-to-Point Races

On more than one occasion, I've seen performance horses run until they drop, exert every ounce of energy until their hearts literally give out and they drop stone dead in the middle of a cross-country event, steeplechase or flat race. These are bruising moments, moments of shock and supreme sadness. They are moments when I've had to remind myself that every horse performs to honor his race. They don't mind having us around. But it's not really us they're trying to impress. They do it because that's the way they are made.

Equine behavior is also an awesome and mysterious thing.

⊣ • ⊢

I realize as I write this that the weeks spent at Clovelly Farms that summer were the longest I had been away from home and parents. While many of my friends shipped off to two-week summer camps in Vermont or North Carolina, I had done all my camping nearby. Long weekends on Boy Scout outings or a four-day model UN program were the extent of my independent travels to that point. But I didn't feel sheltered or unfamiliar with the real world. I had cultivated independence close to

Mowing mishap

home, along the banks of the creek and the boundless horizons of my imagination.

Still, it surprised me how independent I was expected to be in my first summer job. After all, I had known Lars and Gunvor for years. They were like second parents to me. My sister and I had spent countless evenings baby sitting the three LaCour children while our parents went to a movie or escaped for a round of bridge or canasta. A little coddling wouldn't have been too much to expect.

But no special treatment was forthcoming. I was just another one of the lads. If the regular grooms mucked out five stalls in an hour, so did I. If a yearling needed twitching for the vet, that was part of the job. And, on the morning of my third day — bright and early on the morning of my third day — Lars tossed me the keys to the pick-up truck, and told me to get some hay from Farm No. 2 down the road. Never mind that I didn't have a driver's license. Never mind that I didn't even have a learner's permit. Never mind that I didn't know how to drive.

Lars hurried off to other duties without waiting for a reaction and I was left in the shed row with a set of keys and a severe case of butterflies. Somehow, I managed to pull myself together and clamber into the white farm Ford. I adjusted the seat to fit my diminutive stature and stretched my right foot for the brake. It was then I discovered the truck had a manual transmission, a mechanism far outside my realm of experience... or so I thought.

For a second, I was totally at a loss. Then I thought of Far. What would he have done? I asked myself.

"Don't try to guess," Far would have said. "Put yourself in the horse's mind and see if you can understand what he's thinking."

OK. So I could try a little anthropomorphism and try to figure out the truck transmission's mindset. I chuckled to myself and a moment later heard a voice in the back of my head, a low grumbling voice that said, "I'm a tractor."

How many hours hadn't I spent on our own Ford tractor, bush-hogging weeds, harrowing pastures, hauling wagonloads of hay. Tractors had clutches. How hard could it be? I took a deep breath, pushed in the clutch, turned the ignition, waited for the engine to sputter into action, revved the gas just a tad and let the clutch out. Or more accurately, popped the clutch clumsily.

The pick-up jolted, reared, spat a bucketful of gravel fifty feet down the driveway and lurched ahead with alarming speed. I sat petrified with my hands gripping tightly around the steering wheel. The gearbox began to emit a complaining whine, and I shifted gears, releasing the clutch with a little less drama this time. At last the truck settled into a steady hum and churned easily down the farm road. I dodged trees along the driveway, wove through cattle gates and entrance gates. With each turn, my mastery of the technique improved. By the time I reached the main highway, where one of those octagonal red signs brought me to a complete stop, I had the process under control. The sign was on my right. Admittedly, I left a little rubber as I pulled onto Paris Pike, though not much more than behooves any red-necked Bluegrass farm boy. I had gotten the hang of it.

Before long I was back at the yearling barn with a truck bed full of alfalfa-timothy mix and an air of cockiness that must have mystified my co-workers. Lars never asked how the drive had gone, and I never broached the subject. No explanation was necessary. Mission accomplished, another hurdle cleared, another boost of confidence, another small step toward adulthood.

For the rest of the afternoon, I curried my yearlings with a relaxed air. I whistled softly, bantered with the other grooms and hardly gave a thought to my shattered love life. Not all surprises are bad, I decided.

⊣ • ⊢

The time at Clovelly didn't bring my social life to a complete halt, though. Around mid-week, Jack's nanny drove him out to Clovelly for a visit. Or rather, she came along while he drove. Jack had gotten his learner's permit and was taking advantage of every opportunity to practice.

I shared my adventure with the truck. Jack was unimpressed. "Sometimes, you worry too much," he opined.

We went for a walk along the banks of the North Elkhorn after work, seeking escape from the beating evening sun under bowers of willow, oak and sycamore. We passed the yearling paddocks where Princess and Bullhead were enjoying a free evening, crossed the old bridge, scampered down an ivied slope and paused by a wide pool to skip rocks across the water's surface.

"So how do you like working for a living?" Jack asked. "I hear it's the pits."

"It's not so bad. The hours are kind of tough, but you get used to it."

"At least you're not cooped up in an office."

"Or a factory."

"Or school."

"Or Ms. Isaacs' civics class."

Our laughter was interrupted when a belted kingfisher swooped overhead, chattering complaints about our presence.

"By the way," Jack began again. "I ran into Anna Cerilli at the Polo Club last weekend. She asked about you. Wanted to know if you were mad at her."

"She asked about me!?"

"Yeah. Like I said, wanted to know if you were mad at her."

"No, I'm not mad or anything. I didn't think she was interested in me."

"I thought you liked her?"

"Well, sure, I guess. I mean, yes I do." Best friends or not, it was an awkward conversation.

"Then you should call and ask her out," Jack said, matter-of-factly.

"Just like that?"

"Just like that."

"Isn't that kind of against the rules?"

"What rules?"

"You know. The rules that say you're not supposed to let a girl know you're interested."

"Stupid rule," Jack objected. "If you want something, why not try to get it?"

"But what should I say?"

"You'll think of something. It's not rocket science. It just comes from inside. Remember?"

And so it was that on Thursday after work and dinner and watching the news with Gunvor and Lars, I slipped into a back room and picked up the telephone. My hand trembled as I dialed the five numbers, my heart hammered, my tongue thickened. At last the ringing stopped and I heard a voice at the other end.

"Hello."

"Er...Is Anna home?"

"Yes, just a minute."

Another interminable pause. More trembling, hammering, thickening. Then, a reprieve.

"Hello?"

"Uh, it's me."

"Hi there. I was just thinking about you."

⊣ • ⊢

It still mystifies me how girls (then), and women (now), seem able to add another dimension to conversation. When they so choose, those of the female persuasion have a knack for communicating that goes far beyond high school English. The choice of words isn't critical, the turn of phrase irrelevant. It's in the tone of voice. When they want, women have a patented way of making you feel comfortable, welcome, and special.

The Navajos, incidentally, have an explanation for this. In their tradition, language is a perfect marriage between a male component that represents the essence of Thought and the inside of Speech, and a female component that represents the essence of Speech and the inside of Thought. That's why the Navajo treat language with such reverence.

Listening to Anna, I could understand that concept. The moment she began talking, in her relaxed musical way, all my nervousness faded. I forgot about shaking digits and pounding heart and fell right into casual conversation as if this were something I did every day of my life. Which it definitely wasn't. This was no daily habit. This was my very first venture into that mysterious realm of dating.

"So, how would you like to go to a movie on Saturday? I thought maybe we could go together with Jack and Lisa?"

"That would be great!" Anna exclaimed. Not a moment's hesitation, I noticed, feeling a swell of smugness. "Hang on, let me check with my parents."

In a few seconds she was back. "They said it would be all right, but who will drive us?"

A moment of panic. A red sign I hadn't considered. A slight embarrassment. I came to a full stop, pondered both ways, hemmed and hawed, then forged ahead. "My father can take us," I said confidently, knowing that somehow I could deliver dear old understanding Far.

CHAPTER IX

Patience, patience, patience

How easily we set ourselves up for disappointment. At least those of us, like Farfar and me, who live in constant amazement, who figure the reason we have senses is to use them. No, to sate them. As dreamers, we realize we run the risk of rude awakenings. We let our emotions soar knowing full well how quickly they can plummet.

Saturday arrived, and I finished my first week at Clovelly with nervous anticipation. Princess and Bullhead were groomed to a dappled sheen and turned out for the night. Their halters were spotless, their stalls immaculately bedded. Not a stray piece of straw in the shed row, not a tool out of place. I made one final round, checking feed and water buckets, saying good-bye to co-workers, then grabbed my duffel and headed out the circular barn to await my ride.

At four-thirty sharp Far's silver wagon came gliding up the drive. He pulled up and waited for me to get in. I tossed my gear in the back seat and slid onto the front vinyl.

"I'm afraid I have some bad news," Far said right away.

I looked at him quizzically.

"Anna called a little while ago to say she couldn't go tonight. Her parents decided to get away for the weekend...to the Smokies. They wanted her to come along." He waited for my reaction.

Once more, I felt that sickening wash as my stomach flipped and a cork lodged in my throat. I didn't know how to react. I waited for a moment before realizing that no logical response was forthcoming. So I swallowed hard and tried to shrug. "OK," I mumbled, trying to sound unaffected.

"She said she'd call you when they get back to town."

"OK." At least a life raft had been launched. It wasn't her fault. It had nothing to do with me. All I had to do was wait. All I could do was wait. All we can ever do is wait. But, darn it, waiting can be hard.

⊢ • ⊣

The physiology of waiting has always intrigued me. I've never been particularly patient. Nor, do I think, was Far. His outer demeanor was uniformly calm, but inside you just knew he was busting to get on with it. Waiting wasn't on his list of favorite pastimes. Mine, either. Waiting makes me cranky. It sets my innards churning and my outards perspiring. It distracts me, disrupts my focus. Waiting is the executioner of active minds.

Most certifiable hardboots, on the other hand, seem to be supremely patient. Time is rarely their adversary. They have a serenity that defies the fourth dimension. Hours, days, even months have no particular relevance. Things move along at whatever pace is required. These lucky souls subscribe to a fatalism that no investigative mind can abide. They assume things will happen when they are supposed to happen and that things happen because they are meant to happen. There is a determinist doctrine to which every card-carrying hardboot adheres. Not that any hardboot worth his salt would be able to spell determinism.

To me, waiting is just asking for trouble. It's like the old joke that I actually first heard from Marshall.

"I was feeling blue the other day when my woman told me, 'Cheer up, things could be worse.' So I cheered up, and sure enough, things got worse."

Seems to me that waiting for things to happen is just waiting for things to deteriorate. Seems to me that waiting means relinquishing control. Seems to me that only leftovers come to him who waits.

Mind you, anticipation is altogether different. Anticipation is the active savoring of unelapsed events. Anticipation allows you experiences that may never actually happen. It gives you moments that become part of your history even though they never existed. It provides perceptions from a surreal world that can be applied to a future reality. Anticipation should be as active as waiting is passive. Anticipation should burn as many calories as waiting saves. Because good things come to him who anticipates.

It strikes me that there is a confluence between the hardboot's patience and Christian faith. Somewhere in that construct lies a common ground. And that common ground must have been where Farfar and Farmor built their relationship. The hardboot is always willing to let nature take its course, to allow the natural sequence of events to occur. The believer is always willing to let God's will be done, to await the intervention of the deity. To neither is time of much consequence. The end, if not preordained, is certainly beyond our control. On this, both hardboot and Christian would agree. On this one solid plank, Farmor and Farfar could walk side by side.

⊣ • ⊢

Far and Farfar

"You have troubles these days, Marshall," I asked kiddingly.

"Man like me always got troubles," he replied without a trace of coyness.

We bent our backs to the work, keeping clean bedding, forking out the soiled, relaying a fresh bed for broodmares and their foals. Even in those days, mucking out stalls could be therapeutic. It was hard enough physically to keep you alert, easy enough mentally to keep you relaxed. The pungent smells of urine or the caustic aroma of lime never bothered me; they were as natural as odors from Mom's kitchen or wafts from locust flowers. They were Bluegrass.

⊣ • ⊢

There is something of an art to cleaning out a stall, and at the risk of offending the more sensitive readers among you, I would like to dwell on it for a moment. The decisions that go into mucking can be as individual as choice of clothing. Yet there are parameters that must be followed, broad outlines that define a job well done. Part of the goal is simple husbandry. It is inefficient to throw out too much clean bedding. Bedding costs money, whether it's straw, shavings, shredded paper or grass. A waste of bedding reduces profit and, perhaps more importantly, upsets the hardboot's sense of economy.

But a greater sin is insufficient cleanliness. While remarkably hardy, horses are susceptible to a variety of maladies, many of which result from unkempt quarters. Anyone who has ever caught a whiff of thrush, which is basically a rotting away of the hoof, knows how unappetizing and unhealthy a dirty stall can be. Cleanliness is especially important for foaling mares and neonatal foals. An excess accumulation of that ubiquitous pathogen *E. coli* can be as deadly as a rare case of contagious equine metritis.

There are two ways to clean a stable, "picking out," which is simply removing all visible manure and wet bedding, and "to the floor," which requires the complete separation of all soiled and clean bedding materials, removal of the dirty stuff and redistribution of clean bedding throughout the stall. In most cases it is perfectly all right to pick out a stall for a day or two. But any horse that spends a significant amount of time inside deserves to have his stall cleaned to the floor several times a week. During foaling season, mares that are due and newborns should be in stalls cleaned to the floor daily.

I'm sure it's difficult for city folk to understand how anyone can derive pleasure from pitching manure around. The secret lies in the service you are providing your horse. It is a quid pro quo, a price willingly paid in return for the loyalty and effort of equine companions. And there is no doubt that our four-legged friends appreciate the amenity. While not exactly finicky, horses have a distinct sense of cleanliness. They never climb on top of a manure pile to rest or graze like cattle, goats or deer do. Horses appreciate the finer things in life. Just watch a mare walk into crisp, newly bedded quarters, do an inspection lap around the stall, then blow a quick snort of gratitude.

Many hardboots insist that a stall should be bedded throughout to an even depth of at least four inches. I subscribe to the theory that a foot-wide swath around the edges of the stall should be left bare and the center of the stall bedded to a fluffed five or six inches. In the course of the night (or day, depending on the season) the animal's natural movement around the stall tends to kick bedding outward. I've seen far too many poorly bedded stalls go bare in the middle after a few hours.

Horsemen have argued for centuries about the benefits of one kind of bedding as opposed to another. Straw is an excellent bedding, but it can be expensive and some horses develop a gastronomically unfortunate habit of munching on the stuff. Wood shavings are highly absorbent and give the barn a nice aroma. If the shavings contain cedar, there's the added benefit of deterring insects. But forget about mucking out with a pitchfork. Shavings are strictly a shovel option. For a while, shredded newsprint was popular. It was economical, highly absorbent and seldom got eaten unless one of your horses had a goat as a companion. The trouble with newspaper is what to do with it afterwards. No self-respecting landowner wants to defile luscious green pastures with headlines and ink. And we've all read scare stories about finding century-old newspapers deep inside landfills. The simple truth is that newsprint won't decompose in the field and even if it did, it doesn't have nearly as much compost benefit as traditional biodegradable materials.

At Twin Brook Acres, we used a lot of grass for bedding. It was cheap, usually baled on the farm, adequately absorbent and easy to work with. The best bales for bedding contained rough native grasses — orchard grass, fescue, some buffalo grass — and very little clover or bluegrass. Some of the horses tended to graze away their bedding through the night, mostly out of boredom. Queet'n, for instance, never saw a morsel of green he didn't like. But most of the beasts were satisfied with their oats and the flake of alfalfa thrown in the corner. They left the bedding alone.

In later years, out at Clovelly, Lars LaCour developed a mechanism for laying round-baled hay into stalls. A tractor would back up to the stall door with a roll of matted grass about four or five inches thick, and farm hands would lay the stuff just like carpeting across the stall floor. Thereby Lars brought the art of mucking to new heights.

The actual task of mucking out, while not mentally demanding, does require some skill. A well seasoned stable hand develops subtle and useful tricks to make the job easier. The secret is in the hands. A good hardboot can sift through a used stall with incredible efficiency, sorting clean from soiled simply by the weight on the pitchfork. A good hardboot learns that horses have different habits. Some leave their manure neatly in one corner. Others spread the stuff around haphazardly. Some have regular, solid movements that clump together into hefty pyramids. Others suffer from the equine equivalent of irritable bowel syndrome. But a good hardboot adapts to the circumstances. And a real hardboot can muck out any stall without getting his boots dirty.

I blame Hercules for giving mucking such a bad name. If that Greek legend hadn't singled out stable cleaning as a classic punishment, maybe more people would understand the challenge of it, the romance. But Hercules, after all, was dealing with bovines, whose personal habits and sense of themselves is far inferior to horses. Of course, to give the Greek sophists their due, Hercules emerged from his twelve labors no lesser a hero for having waded boldly into life's manure.

While we're on the subject of Hercules (and take heart, I will be concluding this digression shortly), most people forget that another of his labors did involve horses. He was called upon to capture the infamous man-eating mares that belonged to King Diomedes. Here, I think, the Greeks went too far. I'm perfectly willing to forgive a rush of hyperbole now and then, but man-eating horses is a bit much. I've known aggressive stallions to bite off a chunk of shoulder or even amputate a groom's finger. But I assure you the human part was propelled instantly from the horses mouth with a snort of disgust. Only a truly mythical and deranged beast would ever find nutrition in something as impure as human flesh. Horses certainly don't. No, much better to nibble at hay, especially alfalfa, or grass or a straw or a chip of wood. Anything that feels natural underfoot.

Nonetheless, Hercules did manage to tame those Thracian mares, proving perhaps that he, too, was a consummate hardboot. And, from what the Greeks tell us, women loved him none the less for his Augian labors. Hardboots everywhere, take note.

⊣ • ⊢

That Sunday evening, as I lolled around the house with nothing to do, thinking about the movie date I should have been on, and trying to come up with something to distract me, the telephone rang. Far answered, then called my name. As he handed me the receiver, he said, "It's Lars."

"Hello?"

"Sorry to call, but I wanted you to know," Lars began.

I mumbled some response. I had no idea what to expect. Had I screwed up? Done something wrong? Was I fired?

"Princess died this afternoon. Apparently heart failure. It happened very quickly. I didn't want you to be surprised when you come in tomorrow."

"Thanks." I paused, not knowing what to say. "Thanks for letting me know."

I didn't know what to think. Just another horse, I tried to tell myself. I'd already seen dozens come and go. They have shorter lifespans than we do. When they die, you take it in stride. That's what Far counseled. I'd only groomed her for a week, I reminded myself. It wasn't like I'd become really attached to her or anything. That's how you rationalize it.

And then I remembered the shadow of her head pressing against my chest and suddenly I found myself raising my arms as if to comb her forelock gently down her forehead. And the sadness set in anyway, no matter how many times I tried to ignore it. Another little spark had gone out. Another little piece of life. Even after that one short week, I truly missed Princess.

That evening I went up to my room, pulled out a notepad and scribbled a poem about death and dying, horses and people, life after death and life before death. It was an adolescent piece of work, one of those "early poems" that Emerson so despised. It painted cumbersome metaphors out of crosses of straw and single rays of sunlight through a stall window. It spoke naively to the ephemerality of living, to the mystery of what comes after. As literature, it was pretty bad. But I kept the original copy for many years, because on that one night it made me forget about my trivial personal problems and realize that larger challenges lay ahead. It was perhaps my first homage to patience.

On Monday, back in the Clovelly barn, I tacked the poem up on Princess's empty stall. The other farmhands would stop by, quickly scan the lines, then move on. No one said anything, not a word of praise, perplexity, derision or sympathy. Not even Lars. For the next couple of days, my co-workers gave me a little more personal space than usual, a circle for my grief, a simple acknowledgement. Among hardboots, not everyone's a critic. By mid-week, the sadness had eased into the background.

I took Bullhead for a long walk around the covered, circular barn that E. Barry Ryan had originally built as part of Normandy Farm. After six laps, the big chestnut colt was starting to settle down. His head bobbed near my shoulder. His legs stretched languidly. His breathing was steady, deep but not labored. I focused on his shoulder and watched the muscle tighten, then relax with each step. There was good tone in that muscle, a good mix of firmness and suppleness. My young charge was starting to grow up.

"What do you think, Bullhead?"

Yearling

His ear flicked ever so slightly.

I started humming. A Drifters song. He responded with the tiniest turn of the head, and a little skip, that prancing step that is the hallmark of a performance horse. But the pressure on the shank remained constant. Bullhead held the training bit firmly and evenly in his mouth.

"I think it's gonna be fine," I hummed. "Everything's gonna be all right."

Close to my shoulder, Bullhead nodded.

CHAPTER X

Winners can be made, but champions are born

Days passed without word from Anna. I worked hard at grooming yearlings and putting up a good front. I made a conscious effort to shuffle off my disappointment, literally walking tall, deliberately using the few tricks of mood management I already had mastered. I acknowledged that life could not always be like we wanted and tried to get on with it. As the sales drew nearer and the pace in the Clovelly yearling barn quickened, I began to welcome the distraction. Gradually, the impending excitement of Keeneland began to buoy my spirits.

⊣ • ⊢

The Keeneland summer Select Sales has always been one of the best kept secrets in the Bluegrass. It is a place of uncommon drama, the scene of comedy, beauty, surprise and disappointment, where every plot revolves around horses. Some of you may never have attended a sales session. So before we get too far along, let me try to set the stage for you. Let's revert for a minute to that other sport that dominated my youth, baseball. And let's pretend...

Pretend you've just bought the Cincinnati Reds. You paid a little more than you expected, but you're no stranger to big sums. You still have ten million left over, and you figure that one, just one superstar could turn the franchise around. You need someone of extraordinary talent, of hall-of-fame caliber. You're willing to lay the whole ten million, all eight figures, on the line.

You look over what's available. You know the bidding will be tough, because there are other buyers out there with much the same in mind. But finally, you see exactly what you want...

Remember, we're still pretending...

You see the perfect investment. A six-year-old kid! But not just any six-year-old kid. Johnny Bench's son. Bound to be a winner. And, if that weren't enough, the kid's mother is Pete Rose's daughter. A born athlete. The ultimate Red.

So what if the kid might fall from a tree next summer and do irreparable damage to an ankle! So what if he might grow up to prefer linear algebra or zen meditation to the World Series! That's a chance worth taking. The kid's got the genes. It's worth the risk.

Sound ridiculous? In baseball, maybe. In most other sports, probably. But not in Thoroughbred racing. In Thoroughbred racing, that's how it is. For major-leaguers in the sport of kings, it's not pretend. It's a way of life, and it's a heady way with which few would be willing to part.

Thoroughbred hopefuls are barely over a year old when brought to the public auction ring, that is, a year chronologically but about 6-7 years if compared to human development. They're children, perhaps at their best learning age, but still children. The most promising youngsters, determined primarily by pedigree — those sons of Johnny Bench and daughters of Pete Rose — are sold at the summer select sales. For the aficionado, these auctions can provide as much excitement and entertainment as the classic races themselves. Millions are spent in the wink of an eye. Fortunes are wagered on a seemingly insane faith in one's ability to judge horseflesh.

Buying a top Thoroughbred prospect is a particularly challenging and exclusive form of futures investment. The return on a successful, champion-quality horse can be staggering, considering the ultimate resale value at stud. But the losses can also be staggering, tax deductions notwithstanding. Loyal baseball fans will still support a losing club. But a losing race horse attracts nothing but bills.

It's a risky business for sure. Consider the fate of the first two animals sold for over one million dollars at the Keeneland select summer sales. The first was Canadian Bound, a son of Secretariat, bought in 1976 for a final bid of $1,500,000 by a group from north of the border headed by John Sikura. Canadian Bound failed to win a race, and in four starts had total earnings of $4,770. Not even a dent in the debt service.

Canadian Bound was retired to stud where his career was largely unremarkable. He was a magnificent animal, and his owners surely considered him an aesthetic treasure. But monetarily speaking, he was a mere shadow of his former self.

Things turned out quite differently for the second million-dollar baby, a colt by Norther Dancer called Nureyev. Nureyev finished first in all three races he started, and was crowned champion miler in France. He

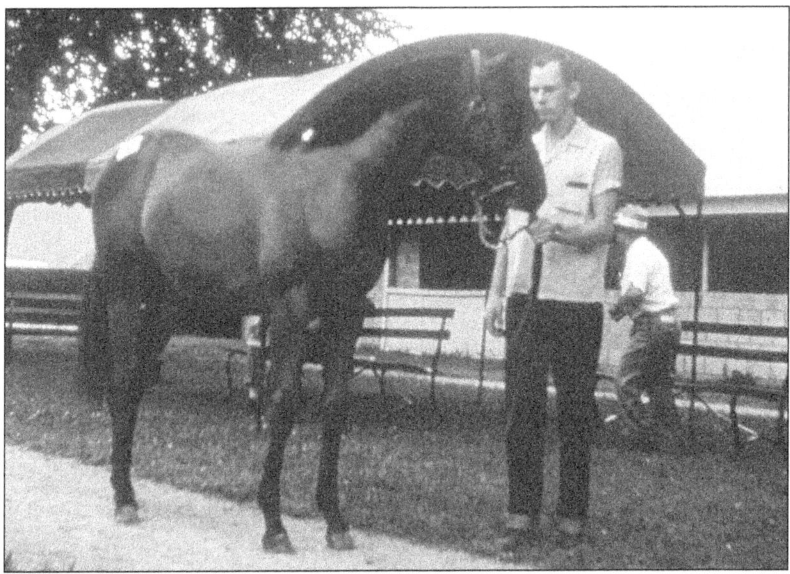

Keeneland sales yearling

was purchased as a yearling in 1978 for $1,300,000 by the Greek shipping magnate Stavros Niarchos, who syndicated the colt three years later for eight times that amount. In his heyday, Nureyev brought in three times his original purchase price every year in stud fees.

Obviously, it takes a special kind of investor to face such financial perils, a horseman dedicated to the proposition that not all pedigrees are created equal, that great athletes are born, not made, that one good child prodigy can turn a franchise around. And it takes unwavering faith in one's ability to see that championship gleam in the yearling's eye.

It takes the hardboot's eye. Not too many possess that skill.

There has always been a relatively small group of people actually bidding for million-dollar horses, a group that includes the most prominent racing personalities from the United States, England, Ireland, France, Japan and the United Arab Emirates. They come to the select summer sales, where they rub elbows with lanky teenagers who groom and show potential gold mines in the form of Thoroughbred yearlings. The few horsemen who dominate the auctions, the Robert Sangsters and the Sheik Mohammed bin Rashid al Makhtoums, have time and again proven that their eye for potential quality is exceptionally true. Considering the risks, their success rate is remarkable.

Nonetheless, not even the outrageously wealthy can spend ten million dollars on a set of four straight legs and a blue-ribbon pedigree without a certain degree of trepidation. As the bidding nears seven figures and progresses beyond, the electricity in the sales pavilion grows correspondingly. The feeling is unique, an integral part of the Thoroughbred industry's special charm. Just a little bit insane. Certainly not something George Steinbrenner should try for the Yankees.

The risks are self-evident for those willing to offer good money for immature and untried, albeit elegant race horses. But even the casual spectator can get into trouble. An inadvertent gesture at the wrong time can do irreparable damage to one's credit rating. If you're lucky, the auctioneers will discover they've got a "waver" and restart the bidding. If you're lucky.

An acquaintance of mine, a young Norwegian lady who readily attracts attention to begin with, once waved vigorously to me from across the sales pavilion. This was acknowledged as a bid of $250,000 on a rather stocky son of Roberto. As the auctioneers proceeded for the next few minutes with the task of soliciting another bid, my friend sat enjoying the spectacle, blissfully unaware that she was about to purchase a quarter-million dollar pet. That the auctioneer and spotters were smiling and pointing at her was no cause for alarm. Men did that all the time. She was, as the Norwegian says, "*sveisen*," which means very smartly "welded."

Fortunately, the Roberto colt's consignor jumped in at the last minute at $275,000, trying to squeeze just a wee bit more profit out of the animal. The spotters turned again to my friend, besieging her with pleas and come-ons. She smiled prettily, pleased with the acknowledgement of her charms, but declined to wave again. The closest spotter actually came over to her and held out his arms beseechingly. But she smiled and shook her head. She already had a date that evening. And so the Roberto colt went home.

I have no idea what became of him. And I never had the heart to explain the incident to my friend.

We brought Bullhead to Keeneland on Thursday afternoon, along with Clovelly's other sales yearlings. The youngsters loaded onto Sallee vans without much trouble. One of the colts had a good long look at the vehicle before walking up the ramp. Bullhead, on the other hand, followed me straight in, as if eager to see what great new adventure awaited him.

I rode inside with the two horses during the drive to Keeneland. Bullhead fidgeted a little on his side of the van and the other yearling, a bay son of Determine, if I remember correctly, made a pretty determined effort to scrape his way through the floor to get at the pavement. But the trip didn't seem particularly traumatic for either of them.

We unloaded without incident, led the yearlings to their temporary quarters and spent the rest of the afternoon making our sales barn as homey and attractive as possible. Flower pots went up along the shed row. Individual signs showing sales numbers and pedigrees for each yearling went up on the stall doors. Halter tags and training bits were polished twice, maybe three times. Each yearling was taken for a lap around the walking ring to give him a look at the shade tent with its corniced edges flapping in the light summer breeze.

Larger signs were hung over the aisle archway to identify the consignor. And directors' chairs reading "Clovelly Farms" were placed strategically by the walking ring and outside the tack room, where prospective buyers could escape from the sun, get a cool drink and only slightly biased information while admiring the sales offerings.

Even with the sale still three days away, lookers began drifting in. A cowboy with a four gallon Stetson and a belly that drooped over his turquoise belt buckle asked to see "that Swaps colt." Out we went, and through the routine we had worked on back at the farm, walking in straight lines so buyers could see how the young horse tracked, walking briskly, so buyers could see toned muscles in action, stopping and standing perfectly still so the buyer could inspect the horse up close.

Bullhead and I came to a halt at the end of the routine and waited for instructions. The looker consulted his catalog, then came closer. He inspected Bullhead's teeth, ran a hand down the legs to check for bucked shins or inflammation, groped his throat to make sure we didn't have the colt on steroids, then backed away a step. Bullhead suffered this close inspection with only a sidestep or two and a quizzical look in his eye.

"Nice colt, but not very big," the man said. "Think he'll go for more'n fifty?"

I smiled as nicely as I could and responded like I'd been told, "Only the auction will tell, sir."

The buyer shot me a disgusted look, mumbled something that sounded like "thanks for nuthin" and stalked off to the next barn. Bullhead and I watched him go, both somehow knowing we would see that cowboy again.

⊣ • ⊢

There were other visitors to the sales barn. Far, of course. I took a couple of yearlings through their paces while he and Lars stood by, evaluating horseflesh, comparing notes and sharing opinions. They paid me the ultimate hardboot's compliment of ignoring me completely. At the sales, handlers don't matter, although there's a persistent legend that a Middle Eastern buyer once hit the roof when he discovered that the attractive blonde groom in the ring wasn't part of the package he'd just paid a half million dollars for.

Francis O'Brien, agent for Sangster, Coolmore Stud and other British stables, came by to look at our Determine colt. Nelson Bunker Hunt, of the Dallas Hunts, inspected a couple of the fillies. Songwriter Burt Bacharach breezed through the barn with an entourage of five or six. I was disappointed that Dionne Warwick wasn't among them.

Even Farmor stopped by, awed and a little uncomfortable amidst all the skittish animals.

"Why don't you buy one as a souvenir for Farfar," I teased her.

"*Kjære vene, han har vel nok å pusle med,*" she replied, meaning he had enough to putter around with, enough distractions to keep him from his regular chores.

"The horse could eat the grass at the summer cottage so you wouldn't have to mow," I suggested.

"*Nei. Gubben trenger mosjon,*" she responded with finality. Farfar needed his exercise.

And then, very unexpectedly, the cutest little redhead appeared around the corner of the barn, calling my name. I blushed and coughed, feeling my hardboot demeanor melt rapidly away.

"Hey," I managed.

"I just knew we'd find you," Anna chirped. "I was showing my cousin around Lexington and Keeneland seemed the perfect place to start."

Only then did I notice the older girl standing next to Anna. She smiled and reached out a hand.

"I'm Carol," she offered.

Farmor didn't waste a moment. "Hello," she said, taking the proffered hand. "I am the grandmother."

"Oh," Anna squealed. "Is this your grandmother?" And for the next several minutes, the two girls descended on Farmor with genuine Southern efficiency, bubbling and babbling about this and that in words the old Norwegian woman could only guess at. But she continued smiling her brightest, every now and then nodding, "*jaså, jaså.*"

Finally, Anna turned to me and asked pleasantly with just a touch of scolding, "Why haven't you called me?"

"I...er...um.."

"Are you mad or something?"

"No, no. I just though you were going to call me."

"Silly. You shouldn't wait for me."

She had me flustered. What was I supposed to do? What did the rules say? Who was supposed to do what? "OK, I'll call," I surrendered.

"Great," Anna beamed. She laid her hand briefly on my sleeve and then, as quickly as they had arrived, she and the cousin were gone, waving energetically as they disappeared around the corner.

"*Hun var da søt,*" Farmor commented.

Yes, Anna was sweet. Sweet and beguiling and unsettling. And as I stood beside my grandmother in the shade of the shed row, it dawned on me that Farmor, language barrier notwithstanding, understood much more about what had just happened than I did. And I realized that in one way, the rules hadn't changed much from her generation to ours. And I realized that some kind of message had been sent that I was having trouble understanding, even though Farmor did. And I realized that, for me, the rules were changing much too fast.

I was relieved when Lars motioned to bring Bullhead out. Right then, I needed a horse to talk to.

CHAPTER XI

TALK QUIETLY TO A HORSE AND YOU'LL HAVE A VERY SATISFYING CONVERSATION

*Begin to argue with a horse
and you've already lost the argument.*

For the next couple of days, I had plenty of opportunity to ponder the mysteries of my encounter with Anna. But no time to place the call. I was at the sales barn by 7:00 am and rarely home before 9:00 pm. Straight to bed, sleeping the sound, peaceful sleep earned from hard work in fresh air.

By Monday, scores of potential buyers had visited the barn, many looking at every yearling Clovelly had to offer. A dozen or so returned for a second look. When they did, Lars made a point of jotting down their names and which yearlings they inspected. As the start of the sale drew nearer, it was becoming easier to tell serious buyers from the window shoppers. Lars notified the owners and discreet inquiries were made about the lookers and how much they could afford to pay. It was a polite game where few questions were asked but a lot of information gathered.

Bullhead was cataloged to go mid-afternoon in the first session. All that morning I felt a growing nervousness. I couldn't place it. Of course, I wanted the colt to sell well. But marketing wasn't my responsibility. All I had to do was make the horse look good...and not let go of him in the walking ring. Straightforward, hardboot stuff. Nothing to stew over. A few hours of basic horsemanship, then I could hook up with Jack, who had promised to show up later in the day. But the butterflies persisted.

Bullhead seemed to pick up on my tension. Or maybe he was just getting bored with the routine. Maybe he wanted to cast off his aristocratic cool and go galloping hog wild across a gigantic Bluegrass pasture. Whatever the reason, he began prancing a bit higher, toying more with the training bit and occasionally giving an irritated toss of his head.

Around lunchtime, I shuffled quietly into his stall and swung the door closed behind me. He eyed me suspiciously from the hay rack.

"Don't worry, big fella. It'll be over before long."

He shot me a look of disbelief and continued nibbling absentmindedly on grass stems.

"Just a few more hours. And tell you what...if you promise to behave yourself, I'll bring you an apple."

Bullhead snorted, then took a step in my direction.

I reached out a hand. He looked first for the training bit and shank. Then, realizing there was no serious work to be done, stretched out his neck and began nipping casually at my fingers.

"Uh, uh, uh," I cautioned.

The colt backed away, then in slow motion reared a foot or two off his fronts and pirouetted gracefully back to the hay rack. It was one of the most elegant turns I'd ever seen, a full piaffe, a supremely athletic move done without a trace of exertion. It was his way of showing off. Just for fun.

⊣ • ⊢

I made my first official trip to the walking ring with one of the fillies, cataloged only an hour into the sale. Another groom had been in charge of her, so I went along as the designated equipment carrier and last minute polisher. Armed with rub rags, soft brushes, mane combs, hoof dressing and Vaseline, I followed the filly to the staging area between barns 4 and 5.

With the sales already underway, hundreds of people had gathered around the sales pavilion: trainers, owners, agents, grooms, riders and sports writers. There were men in suits, women in cocktail dresses, sales reps in tweeds, trainers in cowboy hats, Arabs in turbans and stable hands in jeans. With the exception of the more elegantly attired ladies, most had a ballpoint pen hanging by a cord around their necks. All scurried purposefully this way and that, into the pavilion or back to the barns, scribbling notes in their catalogs or studying pedigrees as they went. A few buyers lingered by the awning tents at the staging area. One Japanese gentleman, who had been to our barn a couple of times, gave our filly another good looking over, before recapping his pen and heading resolutely for the pavilion.

A Keeneland staffer signaled to us and we led the filly into the walking ring, where two or three animals at a time did laps on tanbark while waiting their turn. From the walking ring, you could see the back wall of the auctioneer's stand, which was flanked by two relatively narrow

Old Keeneland sales pavilion

chutes with large rolling doors that opened onto a semi-circular stage, the sales ring where the horses were displayed while being auctioned.

Those doors were the groom's final hurdle, that last opportunity for disaster to strike before the Keeneland staff took over. Many an adult horse, and far more yearlings had balked outright at entering the sales ring. Sometimes they could be coaxed, or even shoved in by brute force. But the easiest way to fool a reluctant sales offering was usually to back him in. Which doesn't speak too well for the animal's intelligence, but does speak volumes about hardboot logic. Hardboot logic builds not on deduction, but on intuition. "You've got to think like the horse," Far always said. "Talk quietly to a horse and you'll have a pleasant conversation; begin to argue and you've already lost." At the sales pavilion, that might mean backing into tight spots, because a horse's best weapons are his hind legs. If a horse has his behind to you, he feels like he's in command. And you had better not argue. But if he's facing you, he's probably willing to negotiate.

Our filly was a little squirrelly in the walking ring, prancing this way and that. But she wasn't in an argumentative mood. My fellow groom had her well under control. When we got to the waiting pen by the door, I gave her the final once-over, a last wipe with the rag and a straightening of the mane and forelock. I managed to get a little dressing on her hooves even though she stomped and fidgeted constantly. Then, in she went, hesitating only a minute as the heavy door slid open.

I retreated to the back and followed the progress of the auction alongside other grooms and stable hands. The auctioneer's voice filled the air with its staccato, sing-song rhythm, blending with the smell of wood chips and liniment and horses. The filly started off at $5,000 and quickly rose to $30,000. Then, a pause in the bidding. The auctioneer went through several pleas for a raise and offered his first warning: "I'm gonna sell her!"

Suddenly, I saw a hand go up across the way, a signal. The back spotter jerked into action, passing the bid along to the stand.

"I have thirty-five, do I hear forty, gimme forty-forty-forty..."

I smiled to myself. The back bidder was Far, acting as straw man for Clovelly, helping to drive the bidding upwards.

Inside, the bid went to $40,000. The spotters quickly turned to Far. He signaled again. $45,000. The action rebounded to the pavilion, where the auctioneer began peppering the real buyer with new pleas. For a moment, it didn't seem to be working. The bid remained stuck at forty-five for what seemed to me an eternity. But across the way, Far looked cool as a cucumber.

Finally, the buyer relented.

"Fifty! I have fifty thousand. Do I hear fifty-five, fifty-five-five-five..."

But in a wink, Far was gone. He simply turned around and walked quickly away, having played out his role, having milked another $20,000 out of the buyer on Clovelly's behalf. And with his departure, the auction came to an abrupt end. The auctioneer gave second warning, then hammered the sale.

"Fifty thousand dollars to the gentleman on the left aisle," he concluded.

I met up with the filly and as she exited the sales ring.

" I didn't think she'd go that high," my fellow groom remarked.

"Nope," I agreed. "She almost didn't."

Barely an hour later, I slipped the training bit into Bullhead's mouth and snapped it in place through the cheek rings of his shiny sales halter. He stood quietly while I worked, but his eyes were dilated and his nostrils flared. He was alert. He was ready. He knew something was up.

We left the shed row and started down the drive toward the sales pavilion. When Bullhead realized we were leaving the stable area, he suddenly stopped dead in his tracks. I felt him stiffen next to me and when I turned to him, I could see his shoulder muscles quivering. He was jittery.

"Easy, big fella," I crooned. "Everything's fine. We're just gonna do some sightseeing."

He looked at me with round innocent eyes, as if to say, "You promise?"

"It'll be a piece of cake, Bullhead. Trust me."

I gave the shank a slight tug and set off again. Bullhead exhaled audibly and followed alongside.

By the time we reached the staging area, some hundred yards away, he had regained most of his composure. The sight of other horses perked him up. He began his trademark prance.

This time, no less than three lookers were waiting, pens in hand and catalog pages at the ready. One by one they descended on the colt, stroking his legs, checking his height, asking me to walk him down the path and back again, up the path and back again, down the path and back again. One man took out a small flashlight and beamed it in the colt's eye. Another poked at his privates to see if everything was in order. Throughout this ordeal, Bullhead maintained his proud demeanor. Even when the last looker, familiar in his beige Stetson, peeled back Bullhead's lips to inspect his teeth, the colt suffered the indignity with composure. Though he did look a little snarly with his gums exposed, I thought to myself.

Once in the walking ring, Bullhead was back in his element. He began to revel in the noise and activity. His ears perked and his eyes followed the movement around him. But his mouth stayed focused on the bit and his head never strayed more than a foot or two from my shoulder.

We stood in the waiting chute for what seemed like an hour while the auctioneers tried to sort out a bidding dispute. My partner had given Bullhead's chestnut coat its final licks and polished his hooves to a black satin sheen. But the dispute inside dragged on. He began to fidget again and tugged a couple of times at the shank.

"Whoa, easy." I comforted.

Then, finally, the hammer fell and the giant door slid open to reveal the sales ring and an auditorium humming with people and activity. Bullhead headed straight for the door, as if relieved to have come to the end of this experience. And then, just as Keeneland's handler was about to take the shank from me, he stopped. Halfway through the doorway. He looked at me, looked at the green-jacketed handler, then back at me. He seemed to gather his weight on his haunches and for a split second I thought he was going to rear and bolt, right there in open view of every horseman and hardboot that mattered anywhere in the universe.

I took a deep breath and murmured quietly, "Don't worry fella, I'm not going anywhere. Easy, big guy."

Bullhead snorted, shook himself slightly, gave me one last look as if to say "you'd better be right," and stepped smartly through the door. Together, we walked majestically up to the handler. I handed the colt over and stepped to the side of the auctioneer's stand. First then did I feel my heart muscles hammering at my rib cage. I forced down a deep breath as the sale began.

⊣ • ⊢

It was the only time in my life I've been in the sales ring while an auction was in progress. Had I realized this would be my only chance, I might have been more diligent about looking around to see what the pavilion looked like from up where the action was. I might have tried harder to spot celebrities among the audience. But that one time, like everyone else in the room, I was focused on the real center of attention, the magnificent young horse for sale in the ring.

Bullhead warmed to the attention. He stood erect and straight, turning his head majestically to take in the environs. He followed the handler's lead with acceptable obedience, with only a tug or two to show his mettle. He looked intelligent, well toned and well turned out. For all of that, I could have been proud of myself. But at the time, I remember being proud of that colt.

When the bidding started, it moved rapidly from $25,000 to $60,000. There were clearly at least three potential buyers vying for him. But they must have been Scottish buyers. Once past fifty, they began asking for cut bids, raising the price by only $2,500 or $1,000 each time. But the price kept rising. It passed seventy, and eighty and ninety without much of a pause. Then one buyer dropped out. I saw the cowboy leave his seat and head for the exit door.

"Thank you for your help, sir," the senior auctioneer, George Swinebroad offered. "Do I hear ninety-five?"

A spotter whooped.

"Do I hear a hundred? Hundred-hun-hun-dred-hun-hun..."

Swinebroad chattered on for a long minute, then fell silent. "All right, boys. I know your kind. How about ninety-seven five?

Another whoop.

Swinebroad smiled. "I thought so. Now let's close him out. Do I hear hundre-dre-dre-drehun-dred?"

"Yeeeesssss!!!"

And it was over. As I reclaimed Bullhead's shank from the handler, I could almost make out a grin on my colt's snarly lips. "I'm worth at least that, he was telling me."

Who was I to argue?

⊢ • ⊣

With the Clovelly consignment finished for the day, Lars gave me a dinner break. I hurried back to the pavilion where I knew Jack would be waiting. We sidled up to the rail alongside the prepping chute, watching other grooms work feverishly with rags and soft brushes to make the young horses' coats as shiny as newly minted coins.

Just above us, the back spotters kept their eyes peeled for bidders. The ongoing auction rang out over the public address system, loud enough to be heard above the general hubbub of the crowd.

Understandably, a lot of first-timers find the patter of the auctioneers intimidating. Even veterans sometimes have trouble keeping up with the verbal acrobatics of seasoned pitchmen, who direct the transfer of valuable horseflesh with musical precision. Bids appear as if out of nowhere, and the dollars flow. With studied tact, the auctioneers chant unintelligible numbers, so that buyers may enjoy the sales without being distracted by such trivialities as price. Purchasing a fine Thoroughbred becomes practically painless.

But it would be wrong to assume that the auctioneers are simply salesmen, or floor managers, or even entertainers. Theirs is a highly skilled profession incorporating all of the above. And in that seemingly impenetrable babble is a wealth of information. The patter provides clues about pedigree and soundness and looks and potential. The auctioneers berate buyers for lack of courage and praise the horses being offered. They paint the possibilities with tantalizing flair, and blithely dismiss the risks.

Jack and I drank it all in. We let ourselves be transported into this carnival atmosphere and were soon in high spirits. We listened intently and began to recognize some of the tricks. Each auctioneer had a special set of phrases that they could repeat rapidly between each bid. Some used numbers, others coaxed the buyers. The words slurred together and melted into a rich melange of come-ons and special inducements.

Like any smoke-and-mirror creation, the sales talk lent itself to parody. We began to joke about the hidden meanings, and were soon compiling our own glossary of the sales jargon, a dictionary for the benefit of sales-goers who hadn't yet decoded the peculiar idiom of auction personnel. I fished out a pen and started scribbling on the note pages in the back of the auction catalog:

"Generous stakes horse." Any animal with lots of seconds and thirds, but few wins.

"Off to a promising start." Any yearling sired by an overpriced son of Bull Lea.

"Get her properly started." A request for an initial bid at twice the animal's value.

"Looks the part." A warning to buyers to remove vaseline, snake oil, talcum and beeswax as soon as possible to prevent skin rash.

"Exceptional individual." Any animal brought into the ring.

"Good black-type family behind her." A shortage of stakes horses in the first generation, i.e. the black type was way behind her.

"You're out in back, boys." Coded message to staff to bring the auctioneer more liquid refreshment.

"Could be any kind of horse." Clothes horse, saw horse, etc.

We were on a roll. I flipped the page, jotting down my own ideas and Jack's in rapid succession:

"Test crop." Any first season stallion not properly advertised.

"Gotta go." Even auctioneers need potty breaks.

"New money." The consignor is getting nervous about not reaching the reserve.

"Soft spot." Where the auctioneer would like to be scratched after an hour on the stand; or, where you would like to kick him after he sells your horse below stud fee.

"Highly regarded." Owned by any Keeneland board member.

"Worth the money if you never hang the tack on her." An appeal to rich physicians with teenage daughters and large back yards."

"Only a late May foal." A reminder that the buyer won't have to worry about nomination fees to the Derby.

"Are you finished?" A question to determine whether all the bidders have come to their senses.

—ⵏ • ⵏ—

In the end, Jack and I were laughing so hard the spotters began casting irritated looks in our direction. Still struggling to hold back laughter, we slapped our catalogs shut and retreated into the hallway, away from the action, away from the infectious excitement and pageantry of the world's greatest horse auction.

I was still glowing from the day's excitement when Jack, freshly printed driver's license in hand, dropped me off at the house. I was happy; I was content. Something about the day's events had bolstered my confidence. I tossed my jacket onto a chair in the hallway and, even though it was getting late, went straight for the telephone.

CHAPTER XII

KNOW THE PECKING ORDER

We talked for what seemed like hours. I told her about the sales. She told me all about her trip to the Smokies. I talked a little about Viking. She told me all about her cousin's visit. I stammered out the story of my first encounter with a standard transmission. She told me all about a game of tag at the Polo Club. After a while, I gave up trying to match her loquaciousness. I leaned back with the receiver stuck to my ear listening to her sweet, enthusiastic patter.

The conversation was finally brought to a halt by Mr. Cerilli, whose voice intruded in the background, suggesting the phone line had been tied up long enough.

"Dad says I have to hang up now. Call me again?"

As if there were any doubt. "Sure, but what about that movie?"

"I don't think we can right now. It's so busy. Wish we could." She sounded genuinely disappointed...much to my satisfaction. But that was not what I wanted to hear...much to my dissatisfaction. "This weekend and next weekend are pretty tied up. Don't worry though; we'll get to it sometime. It's not like we won't see each other. Bye now. Gotta run."

⊢ • ⊣

I tried not to take it too heavily. She was right. We would see each other each weekend over the next few weeks. With summer drawing to a close, the horse world was getting busy. Late July through early September was the peak of the show season. And horse shows were a time-consuming activity for riders, parents, horses and friends. And Anna's parents jealously guarded their family time. Not much chance for socializing on horse show weekends.

To complicate matters, I now had at least three horses to exercise. Gray Smoke shipped in the very next morning. Viking needed regular workouts to keep his belly in check. And I was working with Gay Blade, the dressage specialist, for a Mounted Troop performance.

Our first stop would be the Lexington Junior League Horse Show, a classy, bustling competition that stretched over a whole week. Originally created as a showcase for gaited horses, the Junior League had expanded to include hunters and jumpers. Far played a small role in making that happen, but most of the credit went to J.T. Denton, who for years managed the event for the Lexington Junior League, the women's service club that ran the show as an annual fundraiser.

Combined shows for gaited horses and hunters were a novelty back then. The saddlebred crowd had its own circuit that included many county fairs in the Bluegrass and culminated in the Junior League and the State Fair in Louisville. A few fairs began offering classes for so-called "forward seat" equitation as the English style of riding and competition over jumps became more and more popular. But the Junior League remained the first and biggest event where the vastly different horse cultures came together.

Everything from Hackney ponies to Tennessee Walking Horses to Percherons to American Saddlebred to Trachaner/Thoroughbred crosses gathered at the Red Mile. The show lasted for two weeks, with junior classes and equitation over jumps in the afternoons and formal three-gaited and five-gaited qualifiers in the evenings. Grand championships were held on Friday and Saturday evenings, and no fancier display of horses, riders or tack could be found anywhere than on those electric nights.

The Junior League was a horse show with the emphasis on show. Turn-out was everything. Appearance was paramount. If it was going in the show ring, it was polished. Horses' coats shimmered like satin in the lights, every piece of leather rubbed with neatsfoot oil to a high gloss, every carriage and sulky buffed so bright they reflected tomorrow. And the riders were always dressed to the nines, usually with habits bought for the occasion, tailored jodhpurs and waistcoats, English leather boots, ties held in place with heavy gold pins.

⊣ • ⊢

This particular year, the Lexington Mounted Troop had been booked to present the colors at the formal opening Friday evening. And everything had been readied to meet Junior League standards. The horses were turned out beautifully, the tack buffed, equipment polished. That afternoon Marshall, Randy and I loaded the four academy horses — Gay Blade, Silver Jim, Cub Scout and Sergeant — that would be participating in the event. Jack and Rab had already shipped their own horses to the grounds a couple of days earlier and would meet us there.

"Know the pecking order," Marshall would say as we led the horses to the loading ramp. Gay Blade first, the proud saddlebred. Silver Jim next, the quiet, dignified performer. Both walked easily into a Sallee van and headed off to the show grounds.

"Know the pecking order," Randy echoed. Cub Scout, the clown of the herd, a welcome companion with no leadership ambitions, shuffled awkwardly into the farm trailer. And finally, we loaded Sergeant, the lethargic veteran. All Sergeant asked of life was to be pointed in the right direction and be fed regularly.

We arrived at the Red Mile as the sun settled behind the grandstand. It was a mild evening with a few wispy clouds that shimmered pink and aqua in the twilight. The show was set to start at dusk, so we had just enough time to saddle up and run the horses through some simple exercises to ease their jitters. There were seven members of the troop who turned out for this unusual gig, all dressed in sharply pressed gray uniforms with navy blue trim and epaulets. We mounted and assembled in the infield, our dress sabres clinking softly against the tack, lance pennants fluttering in the breeze. We milled around, chatting about trivialities and enjoying the camaraderie.

"You gonna stick around for a while afterwards?" I asked Jack.

"Guess so. You?"

"Unless Far needs me to go back with the horses," I responded, although I suspected that Randy and Marshall could cover those duties.

Finally, the ringmaster gave us the signal. We raised the colors and moved smartly into the show ring, Gay Blade at the lead with three pairs of riders in close-order formation right behind. We executed a snappy series of drills practiced for weeks at the academy, including an alternating cross-over that even Cub Scout took seriously. The tattoo went beautifully. At one point, the horses were moving in such unison that their hoofbeats became a single muffled cadence in the soft sand of the show ring. Gay Blade led proudly and Sergeant followed dutifully. It was a routine that even the RCMP would have applauded.

The troop concluded its performance with a full canter lap around the ring, then riders peeled off one by one and came to an abrupt halt in front of the grandstand. There was some frantic whispering while we edged the horses into formation and straightened the flags. Then the command, "Ten-hut!"

As the organist intoned the first notes of the national anthem, we snapped to and drew our sabres in salute. I remember sitting there at attention on Gay Blade and suddenly realizing how big the crowd was, maybe a thousand spectators in the stands and lining the perimeter of the show ring. This was a lot more people than usually came to hunt seat events in the daytime. Had I known how big the audience was going to be, it might have rattled me. Now it was too late. The performance was over and had gone well. The guys in gray were all troopers. They'd done the drill a hundred times and each rider knew his mount's moods and idiosyncrasies and strengths and weaknesses.

Looking out, I recognized a few acquaintances. Marshall was off to one side with a big grin on his face. Farmor, Mom and Vera were right up front, being duly supportive. Also at the rail was a familiar gray-haired farmer dressed in overalls and carrying a five-foot walking stick. He was a regular at the Junior League, a colorful character who hiked along the roads from Mercer County every day to watch the horse show. And strolling haughtily through the crowd was the unrivaled diva of the gaited horse set, Miss Mary Ann Wyse, her twin poodles dyed precisely to match her cerise summer dress.

The moment seemed to last forever. The Star Spangled Banner droned on as the horses got more and more fidgety under us. Cub Scout began casting nervous glances at the flags waving only inches from his head. Even the phlegmatic Sergeant shifted his weight from side to side. But eventually the rocket's red glare faded and the Lexington Mounted Troop trotted in single file out of the limelight and into the gathering darkness where Far and other parents stood waiting with a sense of pride tinged with relief.

⊣ • ⊢

Far rewarded me for a job well done with a couple of hours off. "Enjoy the show for a while," he suggested. I didn't need to be asked twice. Once the horses were homeward bound, Jack and I set out to take in the ambiance.

There was a good bit of friendly rivalry between hunt seat folks and gaited folks. We made fun of the heavy training shoes the gaited horses wore, and their set tails that usually flipped off to one side exposing a well cleansed but hardly delicate anus. We used to say that if the gaited girls spent as much time practicing canter leads as they did fixing their hair nets, they might make decent riders.

But the ribbing didn't go very deep. To the contrary, we sometimes crossed that great divide of equine culture and made friends with some of the saddlebred crowd. This year, Jack was keen to go one step further. There was a pair of twins from the Cincinnati area that always came to the Junior League, the one cuter than the other. That summer, Jack was spending a lot of time with Jill and Cathy May.

More than once, my friend came close to making a total fool of himself over Cathy. If she was on the grounds, you could bet Jack was not far away. He helped her load and unload, tack and untack, mount and dismount and remount. He hot-walked her horse while cooling his own heels, always at her beck and call. Jack even offered to polish Cathy's boots. But the May family needed no assistance in the shoeshine department. There was enough help around to serve their every need. Between the farm manager and the stable hands, the butler and the mother's personal secretary, it was a very well serviced May entourage.

And as much as Jack wanted to be part of the goings-on, Cathy would have nothing of it. She chastised him for "being such a pest," while motioning effortlessly for the stable boy to help remove her boots. And Jack would stand off to the side with a doleful look, wishing it was him sliding the fine leather off her slender foot.

The rest of us found this display immensely amusing.

So it wasn't long before we set out toward the barn where the May's string of three-gaited and five-gaited champions were stabled. As fate would have it, both Jill and Cathy were there. They were dressed in riding togs, but apparently had some time before they were scheduled to compete. The hair nets and riding hats were not yet tucked impeccably in place.

Jill was in an impish mood. "Oh, look Cathy. It's your suitor."

"Puhleeease!" Cathy moaned.

To his credit, Jack remained unfazed. "Hello again," he grinned.

I said nothing. But Jill sauntered up to me, took my arm, fixed her brown eyes straight at me, and asked, "Should we leave them alone?"

I said nothing. I had no clue what to say.

"Don't you dare!" Cathy protested.

Jill linked her arm through mine and turned coquettishly to her sister. "Well, we're going to look at tack rooms. You two can do as you please."

Cathy was left with no alternative. "All right. We'll come, too," she said peevishly, making it clear that she had no intention of entertaining Jack desCognets all by herself.

I was certainly in no position to protest.

⊣ • ⊢

To this day, I have no clue why Jill May chose that particular evening to flirt with me. Maybe she liked a man (I use the term facetiously) in uniform. Doubtful. Blue epaulets notwithstanding, the uniform wasn't that fancy. Or maybe she had been impressed with the Mounted Troop's performance, though she didn't say anything about it. Maybe she had some special reason to tease her sister. Or maybe she simply got a kick out of leading me on. I don't know. It was one of the small mysteries that will remain forever unresolved.

What I have learned with time is that all of us derive occasional enjoyment from the exercise of power. It pleases us that we can make other people do things. It intrigues us that we can shape opinions. It fascinates us that we can create moods. Some of us become enthralled with this power. Some of us become manipulative. And with time, I've learned to recognize this behavior for what it is. Not so back in 1959.

I stumbled obediently alongside Jill May as we went touring the Red Mile. Today, a tack room tour may sound a bit strange. But at the time, it was an integral part of the Junior League experience. The competition for the fanciest tack room was as intense as any show ring face-off. A dozen major stables vied year to year to outdo each other with the splendor of their displays. Tack room walls were lined with velvet drapes and capped with scalloped fabric molding. Floors were carpeted. Everything was decorated in each stable's signature colors. Saddle racks and bridle hooks carved from teak or mahogany were fastened in perfect sequence across the walls.

No piece of leather or metal entered the room unless it had been cleaned and polished. Elegant antique armoires were brought in to hold clothing and other equipment. Many of the tack rooms had exquisitely framed photographs or even oil portraits of the stable's most notable champions. And there was always a place of honor for the trophies and ribbons brought home during the show, arrayed in fancy glass cases, or on special display tables smack in the middle of the room.

These tack rooms were the pride of the gaited horse elite. Their banners and nameplates read like an honor roll of the people who sustained the sport through its golden era: the Dodges, the Phelps, the Teaters, the Abercrombies. Even the Mays, relative newcomers to the sport, got caught up in this competition. For Mrs. May, it became almost an obsession. Who won the best tack room award interested her far more than who won the five-gaited grand championship. Each year she invested in fancier drapes and fancier furniture in hopes of entering the pantheon. Regrettably, she never succeeded, although thanks to the twins, the display of trophies and ribbons grew visibly with each year.

⊣ • ⊢

In the course of the ensuing hour, as Jack and I strolled around with the Mays, a couple of interesting things happened. I decided that being shepherded around from stable to stable by Jill May was an altogether pleasant experience. So I turned myself over to this gaited cicerone, laughing good-naturedly at her jibes and savoring every time she touched my arm. I also began to envy her confidence, her command of the situation, indeed her command of me. I began to relax, not because her manner put me at ease, but because I realized she wasn't being serious.

Another strange conversion was taking place between Cathy and Jack. She, too, began to relax. She also discovered, or perhaps admitted to herself, that Jack had his strong points. For one, he was an accomplished equestrian. She began asking him things about horses, swapping stories and training tips and comparing riding styles. For a while, their exchange bordered on a normal conversation. Listening to them, it occurred to me that Cathy's perceived iciness was actually a mask. She wasn't nearly as socially adept as we had been led to believe. She kept people at a distance because she wasn't really sure how to handle them up close. In some ways, she was Jill's exact opposite.

I was standing in the Teater barn admiring a beautifully crafted and immaculately polished roadster when it dawned on me that even twins can be totally different.

I looked up at Jill with a smile that must have puzzled her. She was rambling on about some hotel in Louisville where they stayed for the State Fair, the Seelbach or something. I wasn't really listening.

"What?" she said.

"Nothing," I responded, aware that the grin was still on my face. For a moment I had regained the upper hand.

And then, at that same instant, movement down the shed row caught my eye. Something familiar. I peered into the dim light. It was another couple touring the barns, arm in arm, talking animatedly. I looked around for Jack and Cathy and found them right behind us. I looked back down the shed row.

The couple paused in the light from a distant tack room, and my grin vanished into the night air.

It was Melissa Turner, her radiance matching the brightness of the decorated room. But it was not Randy basking in her glow. It was another guy. A stranger. Definitely not Randy.

For some subconscious reason, I turned quickly away.

"What is it?" Jill asked, now totally befuddled.

"Nothing," I rasped. "Maybe we should head back. They'll be calling your class soon."

"All right," Jill nodded, sensing that she had momentarily lost the upper hand.

"But hey," I managed. "Thanks for the tour."

"Think nothing of it," she replied with a trace of that May haughtiness that I still recall fondly.

⊣ • ⊢

As Jack and I made our way back to the grandstand, he asked about my change of mood and wondered if Jill's flirtatiousness had scared me.

"What happened?" he suggested. "You choke?"

"Nope," I replied. "Just getting to know the pecking order."

CHAPTER XIII

FENCES KEEP SOME IN AND SOME OUT

Like most of my four-legged charges, I didn't much care which paddock I was in, so long as the human equivalents of succulent grass and fresh water were available. What I didn't realize at the time was that boundaries were rapidly being set. For Randy, for me. Maybe for all of us. In a way we were exploring our fence lines, as any newly released adolescents would do.

Knowing the basics of good fences is a hardboot must. The true horseman can hold his own in a discussion of the relative advantages of a four-plank over a diamond mesh. Or the best way of nailing battens. Or the proper placement of a gate. It comes with the territory.

In many ways, this was new territory, a comfortable yet strange land that I was eager to learn anew. I watched it closely, seeing how the land and the human imprint on it complemented one another. While occasionally unnerving, it was also quite revealing.

Where barns and sheds are the primary clothing of the Bluegrass landscape, fences are the accessories. They are the belts and scarves and purses that adorn the countryside. And as such, they should blend in with the rest of the outfit, offering stylish accents to a coordinated image.

There is no single type of fence unique to Bluegrass country.

Certainly, the predominant choice in today's world is four-plank fencing with pressure-treated pine posts and oak planking. For the most part, cheaper and more durable black paint has also won out over the whitewash made popular by such showcase properties as Calumet. But the careful observer can still see remnants of many types of fencing tested by stockmen through the years in the pursuit of practicality, parsimony or pretension.

Among the region's treasures are the dry stone walls laid out for miles along some of the older roads and pikes. Mislabeled "slave fences" for decades by urbanites, these were actually built in the late 19th century by immigrant Scottish and Irish masons. And, in the spirit of any good accessory, their purpose was primarily decorative. They might impede an occasional wayward heifer, but few of these walls were ever built high enough to keep out a spirited young horse. So they were erected along road frontage with back-up enclosures not far behind.

In the early years, split rail fences were common. As good carpenters became more numerous in the region, the piled rails gave way to elaborate post-and-rail systems. The old fences at Almahurst Farm in Jessamine County were among the most elegant, consisting of eight-by-eight inch cedar posts with brass bolts for added strength, and poplar or locust rails. With constant attention and annual white-washing, segments of this fence lasted for nearly a century.

Another durable post material is locust, which seasons to the hardness of iron and is highly impervious to rot and insects. In outlying counties of the Bluegrass, one can still find wire fences strung on locust posts that have been there for fifty or sixty years.

Other farmers have been more inventive, trying out metal fencing or even concrete. The stretch of poured concrete wall along Parker's Mill Road (in later years a popular graffiti site for students from nearby Dunbar High School) was erected by Mrs. Hal Price Headley in the 1930s. Apparently, she went to considerable lengths to keep intruders off the property. At one point she got so frustrated with trespassers fishing on the place that she dynamited out the bottom of her pond, sending water rushing through underground channels only to emerge with a whoosh at Kenton's Blue Hole a mile away.

Concrete posts were not uncommon in the 1940s and 1950s. They were particularly useful as corner posts or gate posts. At one point the city of Lexington erected its own series of concrete posts around the outskirts of town to mark cab fare zones.

Regardless of materials used, the true secret to a durable fence is good construction. Modern developers too often lay out paddocks in rigid squares determined more by vehicular needs than the needs of the livestock. Little attention is paid to shade or windbreaks. The old timers knew better. They parceled out land with a view to good forage, comfort, exercise and access to water. Their fences flowed with the curvature of the fields, seeming almost to grow up from the soil as naturally as trees and grasses, and creating not simply functional enclosures, but inviting homes for treasured livestock.

In many ways, Calumet Farm typifies the old-style design. Its paddocks are spacious and undulating. The fences follow the curvature of the land and have rounded corners. The chief fencing contractor at Calumet for nearly four decades, Bill Rice, placed his posts not perpendicular to the sky, but angled to reflect the slope of the hillside, resulting in a fence that appears completely integral to the land itself. The ideal accessory; the perfect place to graze.

—| • |—

Far did his own experimentation. He cut corners by using three-plank fencing for broodmares. Only yearling colts and stallions needed the sturdier four-plank enclosures, he said. He also swore by cedar posts for their resistance to rot and termites. Sure enough, some of those posts are still in the ground today, nearly a half century after Marshall or Randy or Bill or Ivar hand tamped them in place. Far claimed the secret was painting (or, in those days, creosoting) the bottom of the post before you set it. The extra protection buys at least a decade of service, he professed. History appears to have borne him out.

But he never once tried to fence me in.

He also designed elaborate floodgates for the creek crossings. The design featured concrete pillars on each bank that held a three-inch iron rail from which was suspended a wire mesh gate of the appropriate length. The gate was allowed to swing freely so that limbs or deadfall carried by high water would force their way under the gate frame. Marshall labored for weeks to put these in, and they worked beautifully for many years, until a series of massive cloudbursts one summer in the early 1970s eroded the creek banks and dislodged the concrete pillars, bringing both gates crashing into the floodwaters.

⊣ ● ⊢

There was a certain awkwardness in the academy barn during the week leading up to Pony Club tryouts. Far was busy. Randy seemed distracted. And the rain pelted down. For a couple of days, the skies closed in over the Bluegrass and peppered everything with cold, large drops that never seemed to end. Marshall took the tractor and wagon out a couple of times to clear brush from a riding trail near the barn. But he quickly returned, drenched to the bone.

I was restless, confused, and had trouble deciding what to do.

Serious training was out of the question. The only thing possible was trotting Gray Smoke around the covered shed row for a half hour each afternoon, keeping his legs loose and mind occupied. We alternated directions to fight the monotony, but going round and round and round got dull pretty quickly. To stave off boredom, I hung a bucket on the wall and tossed polo balls into it as I passed, like a true Wildcat fan pretending to be Vernon Hatton. The object was to get as many balls into the bucket on a single pass as possible. The trick was juggling six or seven wooden balls in both hands while posting the trot and still exercising some semblance of control over the horse. Not that Gray Smoke needed much controlling.

Five was my record. I never could get the sixth sphere launched properly over my left shoulder as the bucket quickly disappeared around the corner.

Jack, who could always be counted on to keep boredom at bay, didn't show. Always a little finicky when it came to weather, he offered lame excuses about chances of injury from slipping in the mud. The heck with him, I muttered to myself.

Farmor was no help. She kept asking about the red-headed girl she had met, referring to my pitiful social life.

"*Hun syntes å være en riktig god jente,*" Farmor said.

As if I needed reminding how nice she was.

⊢ • ⊣

So late one evening, I gathered up enough courage to call her. After four rings, Mr. Cerilli answered.

"Hi. Is Anna there?" To me, it sounded like a squeak.

"Just a minute," he answered.

A few moments later, he was back. "She can't come to the phone right now. She says she'll call you back. All right?"

"OK," I mumbled dejectedly, and hung up.

But she didn't call back. Not that evening. Nor the next. And again the territory seemed both familiar and new, and the fence lines became more distinct.

⊢ • ⊣

Late each afternoon, I sought solace in the barn, giving both Gray Smoke and Viking a thorough grooming before they were turned out for the night. There was comfort to be gained from those evening chores, the sounds of molars munching oats, the rustle of straw, the whisk of body brush on horsehair, all while rain beat out its rhythms on the tin roof overhead. Knowing the animals appreciated the attention made me feel better. And having a routine to go through made the days pass more easily.

But it was destined to be a rough week. Late Wednesday, as Mom was clearing away dinner dishes and Far had settled in with his highball to watch the Lawrence Welk show, the phone rang. For a split second, I tasted hope. But it wasn't Anna. It was airport security. There were horses loose on the runway.

⊣ • ⊢

So back to work we went, grabbing shanks and flashlights, pulling on rubber boots and raincoats and piling into the old gray station wagon. We kept our eyes peeled as we pulled out of the farm and headed up Airport Road toward the riding academy. The sight that greeted us as we rounded the crest of the hill was unforgettable. Flashes of red bounced off the tin roof of the stable, and through the rain came the wail of sirens. Off to the left, headlights pierced the gloom and veered away, occasionally silhouetting a dark shape in full flight. It was like a circus, as two police cruisers darted in and out of parked airplanes, trying to herd a small group of panic-stricken horses.

Far gave a woeful shake of his head and pulled onto the tarmac. Flashing high beams on and off to attract attention, he steered straight for one off the police cars. The cars closed quickly through the darkness, and for a moment, I thought we might collide. But both vehicles skidded to a stop just in time, and Far jumped out into the rain.

I was hardly a second behind him when he reached the police car and shouted over the noise of the siren.

"What are you doing?" he asked incredulously.

The officer cracked his window and glared at Far.

"What are you doing?" Far repeated.

"Who are you?" the officer returned.

Far leaned closer and his voice took on a lower, more ominous tone. "These are my horses, and if you don't turn off these sirens, they could be seriously hurt."

In the distance, the other cruiser continued its insane rodeo impressions. I watched as a dark form ducked under the wing of a Piper and seemed to trip on one of the tie-downs. It stumbled and then disappeared into the darkness again.

"We're just trying to get them off the runway."

"This is not the way to do it!" Far continued. "Turn off those sirens. You're just scaring them."

The policeman stared at Far for a minute, obviously not pleased with someone telling him what to do. But the sight of us standing in the driving rain glistening in raindrops from head to toe seemed to convince him that we weren't there for our own enjoyment. Finally, he flicked off his own siren and reached for the radio.

"The animals' owner is here. He says to turn off the sirens."

"And stop chasing them!" Far urged.

"Better regroup over here," the officer signaled.

"And turn off your flashers," Far continued.

The officer looked once more at Far, as if to make absolutely certain he wasn't being hoodwinked. Then he relented. "Let's stand down and give them a chance," he said into the microphone.

A minute later, all the cars were backed away, lights doused and sirens silenced. Compared to the earlier frenzy, a profound calm seemed to settle over the tarmac. Only the steady beat of the rain broke the stillness. We listened for sounds of hoofbeats in among the parked aircraft, but heard nothing.

"Okay," Far said. "Let's go find them. You go around to the left, and I'll go over here to the right."

To our relief, the policemen made no offer to help. We left them sitting in their cruisers, comfortable and dry and a bit pouty.

I worked my way around a couple of Cessnas parked near the edge of the pavement. There was a swath of grass off to one side and then a drop into a gully. I fished the flashlight out of my pocket, flicked it on and scanned the area. There, at the edge of the steep drop-off stood a black horse, shivering from fear and frustration.

"Whoa, Sergeant," I cooed. "Whoa, big boy."

His ears pricked at the sound of my voice. I quickly dropped the beam of the flashlight away from his eyes and continued talking softly. "Easy, big fella. Come on; let's go home."

Sergeant let out a long, mournful snort, a sound tinged with frustration and relief. Then he came straight toward me, not stopping until he could place his muzzle right against my chest, as if to apologize for these late night shenanigans.

"It's okay, fella. It's okay," I murmured while snapping the shank on his halter. "I've got Sergeant," I shouted into the darkness and made my way back around the airplanes and toward the barn. Sergeant shuffled right at my shoulder, head hung low, embarrassed and penitent.

In the distance, I heard another shout. "I've got White Eagle." It was Far. And as we got nearer, I could see other shapes in the gloom, two horses following dutifully and quietly on their own behind White Eagle. One of them was limping.

I felt a lump form in my throat. I couldn't make out who it was in the dark. It seemed to be a dark-colored animal, so it probably wasn't Gray Smoke. Could it be Viking? Or Gay Blade? Two people and four horses formed an eerie procession as we left the tarmac, crossed the main road and headed up the drive to the stable. Luckily, the rodeo cops had the good sense to wait until we were safely inside before starting up their cars again.

The horses followed us into the barn without a moment's hesitation. As I led Sergeant into his stall, I saw Mr. Proof head straight for his own safe haven. I latched them both in and hurried to the front of the barn. There stood the fourth horse, just inside the door, head hung low and blood pouring from a front leg. But it wasn't Viking. It was poor old King, that feckless and sometimes ornery beast who had just had his life's adventure and was none too happy about it.

Luckily, the cut itself was superficial. By the time we wiped it clean with cold water and packed it with compresses, the bleeding had stopped. But the old horse was still favoring the leg as we led him off to his stall.

"He probably twisted his shoulder a little." Far surmised. "He could be sore for a while. We'll have Doc look at him in the morning."

Then we headed back into the rain to check the fence line. As we slipped through the gate, we could see the rest of the academy horses huddled under a clump of trees. They would surely have been agitated by the evening's escape and ensuing turmoil, but they seemed to have calmed down by now. We didn't have to search hard for the break in the fence. It wasn't broken at all. There was a gap leading from the field to the riding trail, not a hundred feet from the barn. Usually, three planks slid across to close it. Only the top one was in place. The smaller horses must have squeezed right under the top plank. Gosh knows how Mr. Proof, who was sixteen-three if he was an inch, got through.

"He might have jumped it," Far offered with a trace of pride. And I had to agree. With the right rider, Mr. Proof could clear some pretty sizable hurdles. And he and White Eagle were buddies. If White Eagle went wandering, Mr. Proof wouldn't have let a little five-foot fence keep them apart.

"Isn't this where Marshall was working yesterday?" I asked.

Far just nodded.

"He must not have closed it completely."

Far nodded again. "A simple mistake. Too bad."

Far sent me back into the barn for baling wire and pliers and before long we had the fence solidly secured. As I twisted the last plank into place, Far shook the drops of water from his hat and looked up at the sky.

"Hmm," he smiled. "Looks like the rain is stopping. Good timing. This wouldn't have been nearly as much fun without it." He patted me on the shoulder. "Let's go home," he said. "I think we've earned a little shot of bourbon."

And sure enough, after I emerged in my Pjs from the hot shower that Mom insisted on, Far was standing there with a short highball of Maker's Mark and 7-Up.

"*Skål*" he offered.

"*Skål*," I returned, toasting with my dad past midnight on a crazy, stormy summer day.

"Just remember," Far said. "Simple mistakes can have more serious consequences. We were lucky this time."

I suspect that's exactly what he said to Marshall. Not a word more. Meanwhile, I kept wondering about enclosures.

CHAPTER XIV

TOO LATE TO BOLT THE DOOR WHEN THE HERD HAS FLED

Among the quandaries we all face sooner or later is whether to convey bad news. No one wants to be the bearer of bad tidings. No one wants to be a vector of pain. However, there's a burden that comes with keeping secrets. There's a price to be paid for not telling. Especially if you believe life should be conducted on the basis of rational decisions.

It can be disconcerting to see friends make choices based on incomplete knowledge. When a friend makes a choice you know is misguided, it can be downright depressing. If you're walking around with information that might have changed matters, it can be devastating.

Of course, the situation is totally different if you don't like the person whose secret you bear. Then you can't wait to tell, and watch the look of disappointment or horror or discouragement wash over the face of the receiver. In Norwegian we call it *skadefryd*. Germans call it *Schadenfreude*. The closest word in English is malice, but there's more to it than the meanness connoted by the English word. There's an element of keen pleasure, of downright glee.

But no glee surfaces when we hurt people we care about. At the same time, there is no comfort to be gained from hanging on to bad news. Its presence becomes a distraction. It begins to gnaw at you from the inside, quietly at first, then with greater and greater intensity.

I stewed on my secret for several days, avoiding Randy as best I could even though he seemed unaffected. He went about his duties in the stable in normal fashion, quietly, but efficiently, even managing to joke with Doc Hensley when he came to check on King's wounds, which luckily turned out to be superficial.

Could I have been mistaken, I wondered? No, it was clearly Melissa I had seen. But could I have misread the situation? Several times I tried to reconstruct the hazy image in the shed row light of the Red Mile barn. Each time I looked for another clue, something that would restore innocence to the moment. But it was no use. Each time, Melissa's grip on her companion's arm grew stronger. Each time her eyes flashed brighter. Each time she leaned against him with more unmistakable intent.

At last I decided to unburden myself to Jack, the only real advisor I had on such matters. I chose a late afternoon midweek when we had both finished exercising our horses and were seated on the horse trailer ramp, Cokes in hand, watching one of Far's classes.

I took two big swigs and lifted my bottle to do the city check.

"Memphis!" I exclaimed. "Beat that."

Jack raised his bottle, turning it slowly to read the chipped lettering. "Darn," he complained, "it's just Ashland. Owe you a penny."

We were watching Far run a group of ten-year-olds through intermediate equitation. They were practicing correct leads at the posting trot, circling in single file along the rail. In front was Gay Blade, next was King, still favoring the right front a tiny bit, then Sergeant and White Eagle, with Cub Scout bringing up the rear.

"Watch the horse's right shoulder, Jane," Far commanded from the center of the riding ring. "Count out every time the right front leg hits the ground. Count with me. Now...now...now...now. That's when your seat should be hitting the saddle. Count with me," he urged.

The girl on White Eagle was focusing so hard on the horse's shoulder, she seemed ready to bounce off at any moment. But she was eager to learn. "Now...now...now," she tolled meekly.

"Very good! OK, are you on the correct lead?"

Jane hesitated momentarily, then piped up, "No, I don't think so."

"All right. What do you do then?"

"Change leads?" Jane suggested in a meek whisper.

"Exactly," Far concurred as he paced in a small circle with five riders orbiting him. "Just sit twice. Bounce, bounce, and then posting trot again."

Jane tried to do as he said. But her first effort threw her completely out of rhythm.

"No, Jane. That was three bounces," Far said patiently. "Try it again."

Once more Jane focused on White Eagle's outside shoulder, trying to get the gait sequence. As she passed, we could hear her faint murmur, "Now...now...now..." But she was so intent on watching the horse's gait that she was forgetting to guide him. White Eagle, ever the opportunist, kept cutting corners, gaining ground on the mounts in front. He was almost up on Sergeant's tail.

"A little faster, Elaine," Far shouted to the girl on Sergeant. "Give him a good kick." Elaine did as told, both legs separating completely from the saddle flaps. They whopped solidly into Sergeant's hide. The old black horse grunted audibly, and shifted reluctantly into a slightly faster gear. White Eagle reacted, too, and the sudden acceleration threw Jane momentarily out of balance. Her seat hit the cantel in two quick bumps before she regained composure and began posting again.

She looked intently down at the horse's shoulder and a smile crept across her freckled face. "Mr. Ryen," she shouted. "I think I got it!"

"Yes, you're on the right lead now," Far confirmed wryly.

Out front, Gay Blade trotted smartly along, opening a gap of forty feet back to King. His rider was clearly the best of the bunch. She caught her leads every time, and held the chestnut well into the rail.

Far kept a close eye on the five students, offering encouragement, giving hints, moving each one along as he or she mastered the basics of equitation. "Sit up straight, Charles!" he shouted to the lanky young rider on Mr. Proof. " Heels down, Jimmy," he suggested to the chubby young fellow on King.

"All right, everyone," Far commanded, "a diagonal in single file and change your leads at the center point."

Gay Blade led the group diagonally across the ring, his rider doing a quick double bounce in front of Far. King was next, and Jimmy, too, changed leads correctly, even if his bounces almost knocked him out of the saddle. Elaine followed, stuttered once, then caught the correct lead.

Jane was glued to White Eagle's shoulder as she passed Far. Then, with forced precision, she bounced. And bounced again. And bounced a third time. A smile broke across her face. "I did it!" she exclaimed.

"No Jane," Far corrected with only the slightest hit of sarcasm. "You'll find it's much easier if you do it twice instead of five times. Bounce, bounce. That's all."

Jane gritted her teeth and hit the saddle once...and twice. White Eagle kept trotting along, his eyes glued to Sergeant's tail, impervious to the struggle taking place on his back.

"Excellent, Jane," Far commended. "That time you got it."

The sounds of hoof beats and Far's voice and the panting of the horses as they passed faded into the background. I took a long swig of Coke and turned to Jack.

"You know those rules we talked about?"

Jack smiled wryly. "Ah yes, the hardboot rules."

"Is that what we should call them?"

"I think so. I think that's what they are. Tough and leathery and aromatic."

I chuckled. "OK. The hardboot rules. Do you think honesty, I mean uncompromising honesty, is one of them?"

Jack paused and ran a hand through his sandy hair. "Tough question," he admitted. "Darned tough question."

"That the best you can do?"

"I just make 'em up. I don't interpret them." Quintessential Jack, always blind to his legal destiny.

A dust swirl from Mr. Proof's hind feet took aim at us, and we covered the mouths of our Cokes. I went to the heart of the matter. "You think Randy and Melissa are getting along okay?" I asked.

"How should I know?" Jack replied. A little curtly, I thought.

"Haven't seen her out here in a few days."

"So...?"

"Oh, I just wondered."

"Well wonder about something else. It's none of your business anyway."

So much for seeking counsel from a friend.

"Okay, okay. I was just wondering."

"Why? Are you hoping they've broken up so you can ask her out? There's a thought." Jack laughed. "You'd be so far out of your league, there wouldn't even be room in the program."

"That's not it at all," I objected, vaguely miffed. "Besides, I don't exactly see you winning any Don Juan awards."

"Well look again," Jack crowed. "I've got a date with Cathy May next Saturday. They're coming down for the Mercer County fair and horse show." He paused, "Last I noticed, you've struck out with every girl you've talked to lately."

"Have not," I objected petulantly.

Jack paused, then shot a friendly jab at my shoulder. "Hey, I'm just funnin' ya," he said. "Don't mean anything."

"Yeah, well I guess I'm a little touchy these days."

"Because of the Cerilli girl, huh?"

This wasn't exactly the course I had expected the conversation to take. But Jack was right. In some strange way, the topics were connected. It all had to do with signals and languages and relationships and communications.

"Yeah, I'm having trouble understanding her. She says she wants to go out with me, but we can never seem to get it arranged."

"Patience," Jack counseled, in one of his wiser moments. "It's like your Dad out there. He knows you've got to try it a couple of times and miss before you get it right. You just have to be patient."

— • —

So I tried to be patient.

I worked my horses daily, first Gray Smoke, then Gay Blade, and finally a pleasure ride to give Viking some exercise. The days elapsed in a uniform haze as late summer heat and humidity settled over Bluegrass country. Temperatures inched past 90 in the late afternoon, and settled to 75 at night, making lemonade and shade primary necessities.

Gray Smoke enjoyed the workouts, which never lasted more than thirty or forty minutes because of the weather. We jumped some low fences every day to keep him supple, practiced the "C" level dressage test until he had it more or less memorized, and finished each workout with a gallop to keep him fit. He went through the daily routine without so much as a snort.

Gay Blade was another matter. There was too much saddlebred in the deep chestnut, too much pride. He subscribed to the theory of "never let them see you sweat," which was not an option under these conditions. After a few minutes in the ring working on the "B" level dressage, white foam began appearing along rein lines and edges of the girth, and instantly Gay Blade lost his natural poise. His head drooped. He lost poll flexion. His lateral flexibility faded. His half passes became perfunctory and dull. But he bore the exercise with resignation. He couldn't perform in the blazing sun, but he was far too civilized an animal to protest.

A couple of times I tried to strike up a serious conversation with Randy. "How are things going?" I would ask. Or, "you seem a little out of sorts." But the ever whimsical Mr. Samuels only smiled.

Finally, when I caught him in a relatively somber moment, I tried another tack. "You look like you've lost your best friend," I suggested.

"Too late to bolt the door when the herd has fled," he responded, leaving me shaking my head. Perhaps I was sticking my nose where it didn't belong, I concluded. Perhaps I should simply drop it. I wasn't any good at counseling, anyway. So I gave up, and quickly realized that not having Randy's problems to worry about only made me more conscious of my own.

Nonetheless, time passed faster than I might have expected. One week. Then two, and suddenly the weekend of the tryouts was upon us.

After chores on Friday, Far called me into his office. He didn't motion to the chair, indicating that this would be no long exchange.

"Are you all set for tomorrow?" he asked, arching one eyebrow in typical inquisitive fashion.

"Yes, sir. I guess so. We've pretty much done what we could do."

"Except get a good night's sleep."

"Yes, sir."

"Fine," Far nodded, as a faint smile appeared. I couldn't tell whether he was pleased or making fun of me. "We'll get an early start," he reminded me. "We should have Silver Jim and Gay Blade in the trailer when the van gets here at 7:00 am." My sister, already beginning her gradual withdrawal from riding, would only be doing dressage. But on Silver Jim, she would be hard to beat.

"I'll be ready," I said, knowing that anything else would be unacceptable.

But the good night's sleep never materialized. I dozed off fitfully, tossing and turning as my nervousness grew. It wasn't the riding that bothered me. Riding was straightforward hardboot stuff I could do in my sleep. Riding was second nature.

The butterflies were gathering for other reasons. Reasons like seeing Anna Cerilli, and knowing that I had to ask her why she hadn't called, and reasons like knowing I couldn't stand myself if I didn't get up the nerve to ask her why she hadn't called. And reasons like figuring out why in the world, for the first time in my life, I cared about this kind of stuff.

⊣ • ⊢

The Pony Club try-outs that year were held at the Iroquois Hunt Club show grounds on Athens-Boonesboro Road, just a couple of miles beyond John Jacob Niles's Boot Hill Farm, and catty-corner to the Howard Tilson Farm, home of the legendary steeplechase and cross-country sire, Braxton Bragg. This was quintessential river country, where the softly undulating landscape of the Bluegrass plateau segued into tougher form. The hills became steeper, and vegetation shifted from burr oak and blue ash to scrub cedar and white oak. Rock outcroppings were more common, and wrinkles in the land gradually deepened, then burst dramatically into ravines as Boone's Creek and Howard's Creek chiseled through planes of limestone on their way to the Kentucky River.

Although several miles from the old Grimes Mill clubhouse, the show grounds were a common casting spot for the hunt club. On crisp, autumn mornings, whip Pat Murphy would load the hounds into a trailer at the kennels on Boone's Creek and make the quick run up to

Iroquois Hunt Club

Athens-Boonesboro Road. The huntsmen would gather around Fauntleroy Pursley, venerable master of the Iroquois hounds, all dressed in their red coats (confusingly called Pinke coats for the London tailor credited with their design) white cravats and top hats or hunt helmets. The field would congregate, horses snorting and prancing in the morning chill, riders reknotting their braided reins and making last minute checks of straps on sandwich cases.

Then, with the morning sun lifting patches of dew like soft white blankets from the hillsides, the master would release the hounds. Noses close to the ground, the Walker hounds would trot off in a haphazardly methodical pattern across the fields, gradually heading toward Rankin's Folly or The Bishop's Landing or any other storied corner of the thousands of acres of hunt country in southeastern Fayette County. The huntsmen would follow, then the field master and the mostly black-coated riders in the field. Over the creeks, and across the fields and into the woods and over the fences they would go, in pursuit of Reynard, but driven less by hopes of a kill than the thrill of the chase, the sheer spectacle of the sport, the glorious interaction of hound, horse and human in open country and unfettered enjoyment.

⊣ • ⊢

We arrived with the rose-tinged morning clouds. A mild front was moving in from the West, bringing relief from the summer sun and promising rain by evening. The air was heavy but not oppressive. The grass shimmered with a faint morning dew.

We were a quiet group that morning, me sitting in the back seat, still sleepy, and Randy unusually quiet next to Far. I wondered what the day would bring. My anxiety was evolving into something odder, something ominous yet filled with possibilities. I found myself wondering what life would ultimately bring. I shuddered, and wrapped my hunt jacket tightly around me.

We arrived in a small convoy, Far's silver Chevrolet wagon towing the farm trailer, followed by the Sallee van, then Mom and Vera in our tan convertible. We were among the first to arrive; Far would have been appalled at anything less. Randy and I jumped out and quickly unloaded Silver Jim and Gay Blade. I took charge of them while Randy helped the Sallee men unload Gray Smoke and Cavalier. The horses were barely out before Jack pulled up, alone at the wheel of his Dad's Buick. He jumped cheerily out and for the next half hour, we busied ourselves with preparations while I kept a wary lookout for the Cerillis's American Traveler.

We were tacked up and ready to go long before the silver and green trailer popped over the crest of the hill. The Cerillis were running late. They would be rushed. Now was not a good time, my gut told me. Be patient, I told myself. Listen to good advice.

But anxiety won out. I had to get around this demon. I couldn't wait any longer.

I asked Vera to hold the horses for a minute.

"What for?" she wanted to know.

"Just do me a favor," I pleaded, not wanting to endure one of my sister's infernal interrogations.

Pony club tryouts

She took Gay Blade's and Gray Smoke's reins with a practiced look of displeasure.

Undaunted, I walked straight toward the Cerilli encampment. Anna saw me coming, and what from a hundred feet looked like a frown crept across her mouth.

"Hi," I waved. Maybe too enthusiastically, I considered.

"Hello," she replied. There was none of her usual enthusiasm.

"I've tried to call you."

"I know."

"I thought we were going to a movie sometime." I stammered.

"Well…I'm not sure."

"Why not?"

"I don't have time to talk about it now. I've got to get ready." She turned.

"But what do you mean. You don't want to?"

"Let's just be friends, all right?"

"Well…sure…but…"

Her mother's voice interrupted, "Hurry up, Anna. They'll be calling your number soon."

"Gotta go," Anna said, facing me halfway, a trace of sadness binding her smile. And with a weak wave, she dismissed me. "Bye," she said quietly before turning to retrieve her horse.

I shuffled dejectedly back to my own camp, and relieved Sis of her charges. "You're welcome, I'm sure," she said archly. Fortunately, she didn't have time to make me suffer further for my stupidity. She and Silver Jim were due in the dressage ring.

I took a deep breath and leaned into Gray Smoke's shoulder. He leaned back. I took another deep breath and tried to settle my thoughts. As Gray Smoke munched grass at my boots and Gay Blade scanned the surrounding activity, I realized that some of my nervousness was going away. I wasn't sure why. The butterflies weren't quite as active. Instead, a black hole of some kind had opened in my stomach. It was an emptiness, though not all that uncomfortable. A bearable sadness, I decided. I concluded that I had done all I could. I was glad I had done something, glad I'd tried, glad I'd ignored the good advice of friends. There's a limit to patience, I told myself. When patience dissolves, action crystallizes.

I had sought to influence my fate, and that was all I could do. A person can deal with disappointment when he's done what he can to avert it. I began to sense some calm. I began to believe that disappointment wasn't the same as devastation. That rationalization brought me some comfort.

[And isn't it ironic that all this took place long before I had my first exposure to Ibsen's *Peer Gynt*, even shortly before my first exposure to *Hamlet*, and most remarkably, before breakfast.]

Then Randy was next to me. "All right, kid. Time to strut your stuff."

"What stuff?" I asked

"The stuff you've been teaching me," he smiled. "I'm gonna find out if you really know what you're talking about!"

I let a faint grin creep across my face. "Whatever you say, Samuels." Then, leaving him with my grazing gray, I swung myself onto Gay Blade's back and headed for the dressage ring.

⊣ • ⊢

I have some concern that the upcoming account of my riding exploits might sound like bragging, that these events, imbued with richness of time, might take on a grandeur neither earned nor appropriate. I'm concerned that this foray into the past might come across as an ego trip, which, I assure you, is not my intention. Even in those days, I was, at best, a moderately accomplished rider. I had all the advantages a budding equestrian could want, the finest instruction, access to good mounts and facilities, a family that supported my habit (if you'll pardon the pun).

But the truth is — insofar as we can ascertain the truth (as we've already discussed ad nauseam) — that I was neither more talented nor more skilled than most of my friends. I had the routine down, yes, having spent about as many hours in the saddle as anyone my age. And I think I had achieved a better than average rapport with the horses I rode on a regular basis. Viking and I certainly understood each other, although his malleability could never be confused with fondness. Svart'n, on the other hand, really liked me. His ears would prick up every time he heard me enter the barn, and he would greet me with a low whinny if I passed his stall. Gay Blade, too, seemed more responsive to me than to other riders. He picked up on my signals quickly and reacted without hesitation. And there was Grey Smoke, whose professional approach to everything he did made communication easy.

Had I been more driven, I might have crossed to the next level, as sports commentators are wont to say. I might have used my own special skills to better advantage. But the truth is, I was never competitive

The author clearing logs

enough. I rode for enjoyment, not for reward. I rode because that was the way my life was, not because I needed to prove anything. I rode to win, because I wanted to please Far and Mor, and maybe Farmor, and certainly from a distance, Farfar. But for me, the important challenges lay elsewhere.

Some of my friends were quite the opposite. Jack loved the competition as much as the actual riding. Who won and who lost were critically important to him. Rab Hagin was also competitive to the core. Lisa Cromwell believed it her birthright to stand atop the podium where everyone could adore her. And the lovely Miss Cerilli herself was a gutsy little competitor who called forth an extra ounce of effort whenever the occasion demanded. It could be a pretty tough crowd.

I was lucky to be their peer. Competing against them made me a better rider, a humbler rider and certainly a wiser rider.

⊢ • ⊣

In the end, it became a long, hard day of riding. But also a very successful day. Gay Blade and I won the "B" dressage outright, nosing out my dear sister, much to my delight and her irritation. The chestnut brightened as the sky clouded over. His ears perked as the blue sky faded. He entered the ring with none of his recent malaise. His movements were fluid and clean and elegant and athletic. He carried himself with pride and purpose through every extended trot and every flying change. He was in his element.

Gay Blade's success was encouraging. Maybe there were rewards to be saved from this dismal day, I wondered. As the "C" team competition began, I focused harder. Gray Smoke and I belonged here. We deserved to be on the first team. That's what we had been working for all these weeks.

The dressage test went smoothly. The gray flexed and extended to the best of his ability, maybe not as flashy as some, but still proficiently. We scored an 88, not bad, I thought, for our first go together. But others followed. Lisa Cromwell, 92. Jack desCognets, 87. Rab Hagin, 89. Anna Cerilli, 91. Macy Wynn, 93.

As the cross country began, I knew Gray Smoke and I had our work cut out for us. Far offered his usual last minute instructions. "Keep him relaxed. Don't race downhill, but keep your speed uphill. Have plenty of pace going into the water jump."

When the timekeeper waved us onto the course, I felt excited, but under control. There was still an empty space in me somewhere. It was a space that seemed able to swallow excitement. It made room for reflection...and judgement.

Gray Smoke excelled at cross country. The competitive spirit of his Thoroughbred forebears surged through him every step of the 1-mile course. He raced against time while taking every obstacle in easy stride. I had to check him a little downhill, but he kept his footing. I could almost feel him nodding to me, "OK, you know best." At the logs, he sailed a good foot over the jump. Approaching the water, he responded instantly to my urging, and cleared the pool with inches to spare. His right hind caught momentarily over the straw bales, but he recovered immediately. At the next jump, I paced him carefully to make sure he still had enough left to clear the stacked telephone poles. We rose easily into the air. I may have heard a slight click, nothing more. Then there was only the brush, an easy 2 1/2 foot obstacle, and beyond that a race to the finish line.

I heard applause as we crossed the line, and looked quickly around. Far and Mor were there. Jack was off to one side waiting his turn. He pumped a fist in the air for me. Other spectators. Randy and Vera. No one else. I realized the emptiness wasn't completely gone.

When the scores were in, the competition had tightened. Rab had won the cross country, but Gray Smoke and I were a close second. After that came Jack, Anna, Macy, Lisa, Jo and Cody. Only a few points separated the top eight competitors. The stadium jumping would decide.

There was a lunch break before the final event. Picnic baskets and coolers appeared as riders huddled with their mounts and parents and coaches. Jack and Vera and I settled under a towering blue ash while Far and Randy gave us a break from the horses.

While downing one of Mor's peanut butter and jelly sandwiches, I scanned the show grounds for Anna and her no-name horse. I caught a glimpse of them across the field, far away. The empty spot tightened.

The stadium jumping elapsed like a blur, only in part because a steady light drizzle filled the air. I stood beside Gray Smoke and watched as one after another of the competitors sailed through clean or almost clean rounds. Jack and Cavalier were magnificent, leaving every fence standing and finishing the course well within the allotted time. Macy Wynn had a wonderful round, ticking only one fence. Lisa Cromwell rode better than expected, hitting only a couple of fences.

Then it was Anna's turn. She started off strong, sailing cleanly over the first three fences. She was riding hard, driving her horse with her usual spunk. She was clearly out to win. But at the fourth fence, disaster struck. Anna came flying around a tight turn, constantly urging her mount to go faster. But the horse's front legs skidded. He caught his balance, but his head went up and he braced his forelegs stubbornly. Like a frozen statue, horse and rider slid to a full stop just yards from the next fence. Dejectedly, Anna wheeled her horse around and came at the jump anew. Over they flew, but a hind leg dipped and the bar came crashing down. At the next fence, another problem. Anna's horse attacked the jump, but this time a front hoof caught the top bar. Another knock-down.

Finally, Anna got herself and her mount back in sync. She slowed for the barrels, cleared them and flew easily over the last few fences. But the damage had been done. A refusal, two knock-downs and a front tick.

Gray Smoke and I had drawn the next-to-last start position. By the time we trotted into the start-up lane, a deep rumbling had begun overhead. But we scarcely heard it. Gray Smoke's ears flicked back and forth, listening alternately to me and his own hoofbeats. We attacked the fences one by one, setting ourselves, collecting ourselves, pacing ourselves. He went about the business without a moment's hesitation, clearing three-foot fences without a hiccup and the three-foot-sixers with a faint snort. At the third from the last fence, his left hind ticked the bar. That was it. The second best round of the day.

As we crossed the finish line, I saw Far waiting, a smile spread across his face as broad as any I'd seen. I knew that I had made him proud, and that knowledge made me happy. I jumped off and hugged Gray Smoke and reeled in everyone's congratulations.

Shortly thereafter, the scores had all been calculated. Stoney Johnston held up a battery-operated bullhorn and made the announcement.

"First Keeneland C Team."

It was Macy Wynn, Rab Hagin, me and Jack DesCognets. Only a few points separated any of us. Coley Callaway would be our stable manager.

"Second C Team: Anna Cerilli, Lisa Cromwell, Cody Miller and Jo Dabney. Drew Thornton as stable manager."

No sooner had the announcements been made than the clouds burst. Copious afternoon showers sent people and horses scattering to their respective trailers and vans. Within minutes, the show grounds were emptied of people and beasts and vehicles as sheets of heavy rain descended from the towering leaden clouds.

As we headed back to the farm through the cloudbursts, the windshield wipers beating a comforting cadence, Far chatted quietly but cheerfully with Randy. "The horses did very well today," he acknowledged. "He's a good horse, that Gray Smoke. And how about Gay Blade in the dressage ring! An unusually good performance." Randy nodded and turned to wink at me.

That was Far's way. It was the horses that mattered. But I didn't mind. Far had shown his approval in other ways. His smile was reward enough, trophy enough to mark that oddly satisfying yet dismal day. And Randy's wink was comforting for other reasons.

I sat quietly in the back seat, thinking about the expected and the unexpected, wondering how anyone ever coped with all the strange twists and turns of life. I thought about Anna and about her problem round in stadium jumping. It made me sad. And I realized there was still a big empty hole in the pit of my stomach. During the long ride home, sadness and emptiness and contentedness wrestled for my demeanor.

I would just have to be patient, I decided. I had done what could be done, hopefully before the herd fled.

CHAPTER XV

TWO THINGS
YOU NEVER BRING INTO A STALL:
FEAR AND ANGER

The rain poured down for two days.

On the second day, a Monday, I pulled on rubber boots and raced through the heavy drops to help Randy finish the stable work. Far had just concluded a semi-private lesson and there were two horses to untack. We sponged down their backs and bellies even though they were going out into nature's own full-fledged shower with the other academy horses, and offered them fresh water.

Far headed off in the wagon to run some errands. I crawled up into the loft to grab some flakes of hay for Gray Smoke and Cavalier, who had been brought up in case the weather broke.

Through the patter of rain on the tin roof, I heard a car pull up and a door slam shut. I heard running footsteps and a creak as the barn door slid open. Then I heard a voice that stopped me dead in my tracks.

"Hi, Randy."

"Melissa…" There was audible surprise in Randy's voice. "I've been trying to reach you," he stammered.

"I know," she said. "I'm sorry."

I froze and listened, just a few feet above them. Part of me knew I should say something, cough, or make my presence somehow known. Another part of me couldn't move.

"I've missed you," he said, so quietly that I knew only inches separated them.

"Randy, we've got to talk."

There was a long, painful pause. "Yeah, I guess that doesn't surprise me," he finally acknowledged.

Another pause. I could almost hear them breathing, and in my mind I pictured Melissa's graceful hands on his denimed shoulders, her head tilted as she looked up at him. Uneasiness filled my chest.

"I don't know where to start, how to tell you."

"What, Melissa? It can't be worse than I've imagined. So just say it."

She pulled a deep breath of dread. "I can't see you anymore. I'm getting engaged."

"You're what?!"

"I know this isn't fair. I know it sounds insane to you. But it's a choice I've had to make." Her words started spilling out, like tears on a tin roof washing away the stains of time. "I tried to find a way to make it work. To make us work. But we're so different, Randy. We're too different. We need different things from life. And I know that sounds horrible and insensitive and selfish of me. But I've got to think of the future, and I just can't see a future with you."

Randy tried to interrupt the downpour. "But, but, but..." he hammered at the torrent.

"Randy, listen to me. I've come here because I owe it to you, because I care about you, because in a crazy way, I love you. But it has to stop here, or else it will become something we'll both regret, something painful and ugly and destructive."

"How can you say that, after what we've had together," he lashed out.

She shuddered, her voice broke. "Please don't make it harder than it is." It was a pained plea. But it was honest.

In my lofty invisibility, I bit back a gasp.

There was a silence, marked by Randy's quick, angry breathing and Melissa's stifled sobs.

"I've brought back the bracelet you gave me..."

When Randy spoke again, his voice was totally different. It seemed calm, deep and measured. "No. Keep it. We're still friends, aren't we?"

"Yes, I want us to be friends."

The words stung, even me, like I was swallowing nettles. They were so familiar, so common, and at the same time such painful reminders of my roller-coaster, pubescent world of uncertainty and courage and disappointment.

"I guess it's that fraternity guy...this fellow you're getting engaged to...Curt, isn't it?" He drew a deep breath. "So...do you love him?" His voice had become darker, almost sinister.

Her reply was timid, almost inaudible. "Yes, but in a different way."

"How does that work? Can you explain it to me? How can you love two guys at the same time?" Icicles hung from his words.

"Randy, don't torture yourself. He's totally different from you. He's a good friend. He's comfortable to be with. He's kind and giving. But no one will ever occupy the place you've had in my life."

"Thank heaven for small comfort..."

She exhaled, in a way giving up. "I know it isn't easy. I don't know what else to say. But try to build on it. And try to think beyond just tonight or next weekend."

There was a long silence, and then, somehow, I knew she was kissing him, softly, for the last time.

The barn door creaked again. Footsteps. A door slammed shut. And Melissa drove out of our lives forever.

I hunched down on the loft floor, trying to become a blade of straw, trying to fade like dust into the woodwork. I had no idea what to do, how I was going to get out of this. Maybe, if I sat perfectly still for hours, Randy would leave. Maybe he'd already forgotten I was there.

"Throw some straw down while you're up there," Randy suddenly shouted. "I'll need it in the morning."

My innards leaped into my throat. "Oh. Okay," I croaked.

I threw two bales of straw into an empty stall and started shakily down the ladder. Behind me I heard Randy open the feed bin.

"God d***," he suddenly shouted. I looked down, expecting to find Randy venting his frustration on a bucket or feed scoop. Instead, I saw a huge rat scampering along the wall below me. I stiffened.

Randy came around the corner and looked up at me with an odd, quizzical stare. "What are you doing up there?" he asked.

"I...I...nothing."

"Well get on down here and start turning horses out. I'm gonna try to get that rat."

I did as told, amazed by the facade of normalcy, stunned that daily routines could survive what had just transpired. I snapped a shank on White Eagle and headed into the rain. We'd just reached the gate when I heard a sharp crack coming from the barn. And another.

I swung the gate open, unsnapped White Eagle, and hurried back for another horse. When I slipped through the door, Randy was standing just inside, dangling a rat by the tail, the Winchester .22 crooked in his arm, and wearing a smile from ear to ear. "Got that sucker," he said. "Man, that felt good," he added.

"Yeah," I agreed, for some reason also sensing relief.

But we should have known better. We should have heeded Marshall's oracle: "Trouble always bring company." Our paltry solace was short-lived. The minute I unlatched Gray Smoke's door, I sensed it. I knew that disaster had truly struck.

The horse's fine gray head was hanging, his ears askew. There was blood streaming down his left hind leg.

"Randy!" I cried. "Come quick."

He came sprinting, "S***! I can't believe it! One of the bullets must have ricocheted. I can't believe it. I've shot the friggin' horse!"

For a split second, the two of us stood in the doorway, trapped in immutable disaster, stunned by incredulity. "I can't believe it," Randy gaped. "I can't believe it," he repeated. "Me and my friggin' stupidity."

"You didn't do it on purpose, Randy," I comforted.

He looked at me and I could see the tears welling up in his reddened eyes. The familiar handsome face looked distorted, twisted in strange directions. Huge droplets escaped and rolled down his cheek. His body shuddered and a single rough sob escaped from his lungs.

What happened over the next several hours remains shrouded in a bleary fog. Someone called Dr. Hensley. I brought pails of hot water from the house and we managed to stem the bleeding and wrap the wound with a temporary bandage. Gray Smoke was still putting weight on the leg, which was a good sign.

Before long, Far returned from his errands and was rushed to the barn. A dejected Randy met him at the door, stammering apologies again and again. "I'm terribly sorry. I'm so stupid!"

Far took it all in with his signature composure, offering no sign of his own distress. "We'll talk about it tomorrow. An unfortunate accident. But right now let's keep that leg well wrapped until Doc gets here."

In due course, Dr. Hensley's red station wagon came whizzing up the drive. He screeched to a halt and dove through rain into the shelter of the barn, ducking his head as he slipped through the door. Far quickly explained what had happened, and Doc Hensley, always a man of few words, went straight to work. He unwrapped our first-aid bandages and probed the wound carefully. When the vet's fingers hit a sore spot, Gray Smoke winced. But apart from slight jerks of the leg, the gray horse seemed calm, even perhaps grateful for the attention.

"I think the bullet's still in there," Dr. Hensley finally pronounced. "Let's try to get a picture."

We hurried to rig up the portable x-ray machine that Doc carried along with a thousand other gadgets in his wagon. Gray Smoke seemed reluctant to leave the familiar confines of his stall, but he finally hobbled into the hallway. I tried to cradle the horse's head while Randy and Doc situated the camera and cassette as close as possible to the injured leg. Far stood off to the side, watching patiently, his brow furrowed, his hat pushed slightly back.

It seemed to take forever, in the uneven light of a single bare bulb and a flickering flashlight. Each time they got the equipment in place, Gray Smoke would twitch or bump into the camera. Doc finally squeezed off a shot just as the horse shifted his weight from one leg to the other. "D***!" Randy exclaimed. No reprimand from Far or Doc, who rushed the plate into the developer.

A silent five-minute wait. The four of us stood like bedposts at each corner of the horse, each left to his own thoughts, each brought to this vigil with different aches and responsibilities.

At last we heard the developer's "pling," and Doc retrieved the transparency. His reaction told us all we needed to know. The whole picture was blurred.

"Let's try again. Maybe a little local anesthesia will help." Doc retrieved a syringe and vial from his bag and injected small amounts of painkiller above and below the wound. Once more, Doc and Randy painstakingly arranged the camera and plate around Gray Smoke's leg. As the local anesthesia took hold, the gray steadied.

"Looks good," Doc said. Then just as he was about to snap the picture, there was a sudden loud buzz and we were all enveloped in blackness.

"What happened?" someone asked.

"Must've blown a fuse," Far responded. "There's a spare in the top right drawer of the desk in my office. Hurry down and get it."

Off I raced into the damp and dreary night, sprinting as fast as I could across the yard, stumbling with dirty boots and drenched clothes into the farm office where Mom stood waiting anxiously.

"What's going on?" she wondered.

"Fuse blew," I panted, while frantically fishing a replacement out of the desk.

"Is the horse OK?" she wondered.

"Don't know yet. Gotta run," I said as I rushed past her and back into the rain. I raced across the yard and headed straight for the back door of the barn where the fuse box was located. Far was already there, blown fuse in hand. He quickly screwed the new one in place and the developing unit kicked back on together with the dim shed row lights.

"Let's see what we've got," Doc said as he and Randy stooped once more to arrange the equipment. This time everything went smoothly. A click, a hum, and Doc quickly slid the exposed plate into the developer. Minutes later we had our x-ray. Sure enough, lodged in the stifle a few inches below Gray Smoke's left hock was a faint shadow, a spot just the size of a .22 caliber slug.

Even in the dim hallway light, I could see tears welling up again in Randy's eyes.

"Well, Doc, what do you think?" Far began.

Doc didn't answer right away, continuing to study the blurry transparency.

He ran his fingers along the late evening shadow of a beard and finally spoke. "I think there's reason for concern. I'd like to try and get the slug out. But it's too delicate an operation to do here. Think we can trailer him over to the clinic?"

"If that's what you suggest," Far replied without hesitation. "Randy, get the Chevy wagon and hook up the trailer. Back right up to this door. We'll load straight from here."

And within a few short minutes we were on the road, Far and me in the front seat of the silver Chevy, Randy in the trailer with the wounded horses and Doc following in his own car. Not much was said on the short drive to Rice Road where Dr. Hensley shared a clinic with a couple of other large animal vets.

But I remember one comment Far made. "If it's not one thing, it's another," he said, in a plaintive tone of voice that I had never heard before. I didn't dare look at him or pursue the conversation. In a way, I think I understood exactly what he meant.

⊣ • ⊢

It would be hard to know what Gray Smoke thought about everything he had to go through that night. Doc Hensley worked on the horse until past midnight, alternately taking x-rays and probing for the elusive slug. But each time he inserted his instruments, the metal blob would shift with the horse's tissue and blood, moving many inches up or down the leg joint. And each probe for it threatened to rupture new capillaries. Although he wasn't bleeding profusely, Gray Smoke was losing blood at a slow but steady pace.

Throughout the procedure, I crouched next to Doc, holding instruments, a flashlight, clamps or an exposed plate. Far and Randy stood by, ready to lend a hand, but growing gradually wearier and pessimistic. At least a dozen times we tried to pin down the offending cartridge. But to no avail.

In the end, as the clock wound towards 1:00 am, Doc rose and stretched his aching, tall frame. "That's all we can do," he said. "The bullet stays."

Far took a deep breath and nodded. "The bullet stays," he acknowledged. "Leave it."

We were exhausted. We were still in shock. In a way, we had all been shot. And as we learn when we grow older, scars will always remind us when the bullets are still there.

It was a low point that neither patience nor action could change. Somehow that night, sleep finally brought a modicum of relief. And somewhere deep in a dream about horses tripping on airplanes and red-headed stewardesses offering empty glasses, a fair-haired lad quoted another of Far's maxims: "Two things you never bring into a stall are fear and anger." And knowing I would be going back to the barn in a few short hours, I wiped my brow with rainwater, rinsing away the dread, washing away the anger, immersing my pain in the muddy waters of Hidden Creek.

CHAPTER XVI

Wean on the fourth day after a full moon with Saturn rising

Far was already in the office when I came down the next morning. I knocked carefully on the door and he waved me in. For once, I sat down in the guest chair without being asked. I guess I felt I had earned that right.

"Anything new?" I started.

"Still too soon to tell. Doc was by there this morning, but he said his prognosis is still guarded."

"You think Gray Smoke will be permanently lame?" I was ready to ask the hard questions.

"We'll have to wait and see," Far said, as always counseling patience.

"OK," I managed.

"There is one thing, though," he began cautiously.

"What?"

"Gray Smoke certainly won't be ready for the Pony Club rally."

Somehow, I hadn't really confronted that fact. Deep inside I knew, or had guessed sometime during the late night hours while we were working on him. But I hadn't faced the real consequences.

"So what do we do?" I wondered.

Far paused for a moment. "I think it's mostly up to you. You could ride Viking, of course." He waited for my reaction.

I had to chuckle in spite of the somber mood. The thought of Viking sailing grandly over three-and-a-half foot stadium jumping fences was just a little ludicrous, however much I liked the old fellow. "Really wouldn't be fair to the other team members. He's no event horse."

Far nodded, echoing my judgment. "There's another option, of course," he went on. "You could swap places with Coley, the stable manager."

It became my turn to pause. The stable manager's role on the team was definitely not a coveted one. He - or she - was responsible for keeping the stable area clean and orderly. All teams were graded on their stables, so tidiness was important. But it was a far cry from being out there on fence sixteen, soaring over stacked straw bales at twenty-five miles an hour as the horse's breath and yours mingled with air and wind.

On the other hand, burdening the team with a less than stellar mount wouldn't be much fun, either. And Coley's horse was decent, easily better in stadium jumping than Viking and probably a shade better in cross-country. Besides, luck hadn't exactly been running in my favor recently. Maybe it would be best for me not to tempt fate.

"All right," I shrugged. "I guess that's the best thing to do."

"Good," Far concluded. "I'll check with Coley's parents to make sure everything's fine with them, and then we'll call the rally coordinators."

"OK." I stood up to leave.

"And, Dag," Far stopped me.

"Yes sir."

"We're going to wean the two fillies this morning. We'll need your help."

"Yes, sir."

"And Dag," he stopped me again.

"Yes?"

"I'm very sorry."

⊣ • ⊢

Late summer and autumn bring restlessness to Kentucky horse farms. Yearlings are moved from sales pavilions to new homes, barren mares and in-foal mares are transferred to winter pasture and foals are separated from their dams. The animals explore their new surroundings with lifted tails and dilated nostrils. Shrill whinnies punctuate the crisp air. New seasons mean time for change.

Weaning foals from their mothers is one of the less enjoyable tasks of the business. Even the most hard-hearted of hardboots senses a special tug when fillies and colts, with one swift and abrupt move, are separated from their dams, ending five or six months of carefree frolic.

It's easy to feel sorry for the babies. Their bright, trusting eyes look around for guidance, reflecting momentary disorientation. But the loss of a copious udder is usually forgotten with surprising speed. Within hours the weanling has found a peer with which to commiserate, and it returns to the more immediate task of filling a growing body with succulent grass.

Ironically, weaning is generally harder on the mares. Apart from the direct physical pain of full udders, dams are also burdened with a

Foal and mare

greater "psychological" loss. It may take days before they are reconciled to being separated from their offspring.

It is temptingly easy to read too much into the behavior of these beautiful beasts. That is not my intent. Equine psychology is not a universally recognized field, especially not as it relates to common practice within the industry. But the day has already arrived when learned men with a string of initials behind their names counsel more gradual transition from maternal dependence to total independence.

The hardboot finds this a bit laughable. A hard job is best done quickly, they will say. And they will mostly be right.

While weaning children is not directly comparable to weaning horses, there are some interesting parallels. Final separation is most readily accomplished when the offspring has an active peer group upon which to focus its attention — a sweetheart or college classmate, for example. And it is often harder on the parent. We whinny a lot, paw the ground and manage to get through it, but all things considered, we are not very good at braking the ties that bind.

It may be because we so diligently avoid the trauma of separation (mostly to protect ourselves) that we inhibit our children's innate abilities to adapt to sudden change. Because we coach our offspring in the ways of the world over such an extended period of time, perhaps we actually build in permanent dependencies on a myth of permanence.

The Thoroughbred weanling, for all its transient consternation, learns very quickly to deal with change and reality. And in that regard, there may be a lesson to be learned from that little rascally four-legged animal. Most of life's traumas are, at worst, transitory, and fretting only makes them last longer. A ready acceptance of reality — harsh reality — can be a forceful tool. A willingness to let go of dependencies, of myths and parents and expectations, can be a healthy thing, a calming thing, a maturing influence.

Indeed, the weanling doesn't dream of success, of winning the Run for the Roses. The weanling doesn't dream of running in the Kentucky Derby at all. We, its masters, dream on its behalf. That's why we need psychologists, and the weanling doesn't.

⊣ • ⊢

That afternoon, after moving the mares and weanlings around, we had a Mounted Troop session. As expected, word of my troubles had already spread. One after another, my troop mates came up to commiserate.

"Wow, tough luck."

"That's terrible."

"How in the world could something like that happen?"

But the most awkward conversation was with Randy.

"I don't know what to say," he started.

"It was an accident. Forget it." I tried consolingly.

"It was bad judgment. Under stress." Randy looked away.

"Been a lot of that lately," I agreed.

He looked back at me and placed his hands on my shoulders. "You're a good friend," he said quietly. "I appreciate your not saying anything about what happened...I mean, before I went off half-cocked."

I mustered as mature a look as I could. "I guess life wasn't meant to be easy. Sometimes the rules are hard to follow."

"And sometimes we're ruled by our emotions," Randy added.

"And sometimes you just have to suck it in and get on with hard-booting," I suggested.

This remark brought a funny smile to Randy's drawn face. For a moment, the boyish charm resurfaced. He poked me gently in the ribs. "You got that right."

No one seemed too keen on mounted troop drills that day, even though the rain had stopped and the sun from time to time tried to pierce the high cloud cover. We ran some lance formations, practiced sabre handling and schooled the horses over cavalettis. But even Far didn't have his heart in it. After three quarters of an hour, he suggested we finish with a leisurely hack in the park.

The guys were up for it. We slouched back in the saddle and headed around the riding ring toward the trail, me in front on Viking, Jack right behind on Cavalier, Drew on Sergeant, and Jim Roche on Mr. Proof. We took our usual route, down along the fenceline to the packing plant, around behind the quarry, quickly past the public picnic area, then around the base of the hill by Hidden Creek, trotting briskly most of the way. We slowed for the trees lining the creek, splashed through the rain-swollen stream, then cantered in single file up the hill that led to a pond at the base of the airport runway.

I brought the troop to a halt by the pond. We paused for a few minutes to watch the air traffic, first a single-engine Cessna that seemed to roll only a few feet before rising effortlessly into the air, then a DC-3 — Eastern's 6:20 flight to Washington — that rumbled several hundred yards down the runway before lifting gently into the evening breeze.

"Anybody in a hurry to get home?" I asked.

There was a chorus of "nopes."

"Great. Let's do the whole round."

We headed off again at a trot, single file, with our boots and scabbards slapping the saddles and the blue braid on our gray uniforms flapping with the wind. Viking trotted comfortably under me, happy to be moving with no apparent purpose, limber and loose. I took a cue from my horse and relaxed, too, breathing deep draughts of oxygen tinged with the faintly acrid hint of aviation fuel and the slightest whiff of manure from the cattle farm to the west. There was no reason for despondency, I decided. There will always be new opportunities.

Only minutes later we reached the South Elkhorn, skirting around to the south, upstream from the YMCA camp. I signaled the troop to halt as we reached the floodplain, and scanned the camp for activity. Everything seemed to be quiet.

"I guess they've gone for the day," Jack offered.

On the rise to the right was our special resting place, the giant blue ash whose canopy spread over a quarter acre or more.

"Look at that," Jack said suddenly, pointing. There was disappointment in his voice.

I followed his finger to our tree. Our spot, our favorite resting place, had been desecrated even further. Two new archery targets had replaced the earlier one, and a crude lean-to had been lashed together right at the base of the tree, the exact spot where Jack and I had spent so many carefree hours. The area was scarred and littered, the grassy refuge now little more than mud and trash.

I'm not exactly sure what came over me. It wasn't anger. It wasn't really an act of vengeance. It was just something that had to be done, a necessity like breathing or eating or sleeping. It was a small act of survival.

I suppose a sly smile crept over my face.

"Troop in formation abreast!" I shouted.

The others hesitated only momentarily before lining smartly up beside me.

"Sabers drawn!" I shouted.

I remember a guffaw from Drew as he raised his sabre and a deep chuckle from Jack.

"In formation...chaaaaarrrge!!"

We took off at a full gallop, side by side with sabers toward the sky, whooping like banshees. Our battle formation was more enthusiastic than precise. Mr. Proof, thinking he was back at the race track, quickly forged ahead. And Drew, who was always doing his own thing, veered off toward the closest tepee. But Jack and I stayed leg-to-leg, head to head, and bore down on the imaginary enemy. We roared into the camp with intense purpose. Jack took aim at the archery target on the left. I went straight for the lean-to.

Our sabers swished easily through the air, popping baling wire and cotton rope like butter. We carved slashes in the paper targets and impaled the bales on which they were fastened. We wheeled around and came at the fiend again, shredding the targets and bringing the lean-to crashing to the ground.

Viking was in his element, using his polo pony agility as we darted this way and that, keeping his weight under me as I leaned to one side and another to wield my sword. A third surge…and a fourth, until the area under our ash tree was littered with straw and pieces of paper, sticks, battered feathers, cans and rope.

Finally, I pulled up to survey the battle scene. Off to my left, Drew was still slashing at the guy lines to a second tepee. Sergeant, the very picture of an old war horse, stood steady as a rock under him. Drew took one more mighty swing and the line snapped. The canvas tent crumpled like a punctured balloon.

Jack rode up beside me. "I think that about does it," he said.

Nodding, I yelled out my last command, "Regroup!! Regroup!!"

⊣ • ⊢

As I think back on these events, I realize there are many aspects that have eluded my memory. I seem to recall a mirthful return to the stables, the return of the conquering heroes, kind of. I'm also sure we shared heavily embroidered versions of our glorious exploits with Randy.

However, I don't think we ever said anything to Far. I probably would have remembered. And I don't know for sure whether he ever heard about the troop's unauthorized maneuvers from anyone else. Quite likely, someone from the Y must have inquired about vandalism at the camp. If so, no mention was ever made of it to me, or to Jack or Randy or anyone else as far as I know.

Of course, some of Far's best parenting was silent and forgiving, like when he never said anything at all, or when he shrugged it off. "It's nothing," he would say. "We'll talk about it later." Only he didn't talk about it later because talking wouldn't change anything and it wasn't really all that important anyway.

There is a wisdom of perspective in these matters. Some moments, some events, some happenings simply have their own reasons for occurring, their own justification. Once the damage has been done, it is best to regroup. Once the moment has passed, it is best to move on.

I felt a little remorse, of course. The kids in the YMCA camp weren't to blame for my troubles. But I felt a little better, too. It was good to get the anger out. It was good to react, even if the action was a bit over the line. No real damage was done. The targets would be replaced and the lean-to rebuilt in no time.

Nonetheless, our resting place was gone forever, and in our way, we had signaled our contempt for that small change in our universe. And in another way, we had signaled contempt for all the big changes taking place around us.

Hardboots don't always deal well with change.

Mounted troop returning from a sortie

CHAPTER XVII

It's not who runs the fastest. It's who crosses the line first.

"*Hvordan står det til, lilleman,*" Farmor asked at breakfast the following morning, inquiring about my well-being.

"OK, I guess."

"*Ja, du har hatt mye å slite med.*"

Yep. I'd had my share of troubles.

"*Men jeg har en god følelse,*" she went on.

"What do you mean, a good feeling?" I asked.

"*Bedre tider i vente,*" she replied.

Better times in store. Sounded good.

"*Fra idag av, antar jeg,*" Farmor said with an almost songlike quality that sounded both soothing and inviting.

I had to smile at her cheeriness. "Starting today, huh?"

"Yes," she said, in English. "Today your life again begins."

⊢ • ⊣

I didn't always pay attention to Farmor's cryptic remarks. Like most seers, her predictions were usually pretty broad. And some of her *spådommer* were just a little too odd to take seriously. And then there was the language problem. But I had to admit, she had a funny lilt to her voice that day.

After morning chores, I went with Far to check on Gray Smoke. We pulled up to the clinic and walked into the stable where Doc Hensley was already waiting. The gray horse was munching contentedly on hay.

Far took a close look at the bandaged wound, felt for inflammation around fetlock and hock, then inspected the horse's eyes and nostrils. He was smiling when he stepped back. "You know what," he said. "I think this old booger is going to be just fine." He turned to Doc, "What do you think?"

Hensley replied in his usual laconic manner, "Still guarded. But good so far."

The horse eyed us calmly and shifted his weight off the injured foot. There was scarcely a trace of discomfort. No wince. No jerk.

"Bill Shorter has been very understanding," Far went on, being more talkative than usual, maybe using Doc's presence to keep me informed. "Of course we'll care for the horse until he's completely sound."

Doc Hensley smiled. "Always nice to be around optimists," he said. "How's your stable hand taking it?"

"Over the shock, I think. He's a good lad; he's learned a tough lesson."

For sure, I thought to myself. And he wasn't alone.

⊣ • ⊢

We were back at the house for lunch when the phone rang. Farmor was sitting in a big chair in the library, knitting basket close by, fingers and pins twirling away.

"*Kanskje til deg,*" she said absently.

Far picked up. "It's for you," he said, handing me the receiver.

"Hello?"

"Hi. It's Anna."

I gulped. "Hang on. Let me get the other phone," I stammered. Passing Farmor on my way to the other room, I could have sworn she winked at me. Once safely ensconced in the den, I picked up the phone again.

"Hey, it's great to hear from you," I started.

"Good to talk to you, too," she said, then added, "I've missed you."

"Yeah, well, me too." I was having trouble finding words.

"It was so sad to hear what happened to Gray Smoke."

"Yeah. Bizarre wasn't it. But he's doing all right. We were at the clinic this morning checking on him."

"And it's terrible that you won't get to ride at the rally."

"I guess," I said cavalierly. "Probably wouldn't have done very well anyway." In the back of my mind, I realized that word travelled fast in the horse world.

"Oh, don't be silly. You're one of the best."

It felt delightfully good to hear her say that.

"You don't mean that," I offered modestly.

"You know I do," she demanded. "I swear sometimes you don't listen to me."

"No, no. I do, I do," I hastened. "I'm listening now. Honest."

"Good. Because I need to apologize to you."

"What for?"

"A misunderstanding, I think. I hope."

"What misunderstanding?"

"I was mad at you and I shouldn't have been and I'm sorry."

"What are you talking about, Anna?"

"Well, can I ask you a question first?"

"Sure. What about?"

"Are you dating Jill May?"

"What!?"

"She said you were."

"What!!??"

"She waltzed right up to me at the Mercer County show and told me she really liked you and that you were going together."

My jaw dropped halfway to the floor. "That's crazy," I objected. "Why would she say a thing like that?"

Anna's voice took on more than a touch of sarcasm. "Well Mr. Genius, maybe because she really does like you."

I pushed past all the things that had happened the last weeks, past the hurt and the surprises and the rain and disasters, back to the night at the Junior League. "You know my number," Jill had said. "Call me sometime. Cincinnati's not too far away." I hadn't thought much of it. I'd been flattered, but it hadn't crossed my mind that Jill really meant it. I figured she said things like that to all the guys she teased with her big round eyes and fluttering lashes.

I realized I hadn't said anything for a while. I also realized there was a big opportunity staring me in the face. I swallowed hard.

"Anna," I began. "You're the one I care about. You're the one I enjoy being with."

There was a strange sound at the other end of the line. Maybe a sigh, maybe a sob. When Anna spoke again, there was a frog in her voice. "Well you sure don't do a very good job of showing it. But that's all right. If you forgive me for acting silly, I'll forgive you. Deal?"

"Deal."

"So when are you going to take me to a movie?" she asked.

"Maybe never. There's too many horse shows," I joked lamely. "Maybe I can bring some popcorn to the rally this weekend."

She laughed her amazingly infectious laughter. "I'd like that very much," she said. "And a box of Milk Duds, please."

"Done deal," I acknowledged. "And you know what else?"

"No. What?"

"I'll spring for a Coke, too. If that's all right?"

"That would be very all right."

⊣ • ⊢

We talked for a little while longer, about horses and friends mostly. We stayed away from the tough stuff, the strange occurrences that our immaturity was having such difficulty dealing with. I didn't ask what had prompted her to call. She didn't offer an explanation. Perhaps one wasn't needed.

⊢ • ⊣

And so we near the end of our little story about memories and maturity and myths and mudders. There are some loose ends to tie up, of course, the most important being the Pony Club rally, which turned out to be quite an event. But I'm getting ahead of myself.

Later that evening, as we sat on the front porch listening to cicadas and tree frogs, with Farmor putting the finishing touches on a pair of rag socks, I asked her if she really thought she could see into the future.

"*Tja. Fremtiden er så mangt,*" she said noncommittally.

"I'm not sure I'd want to know what's going to happen," I offered.

"No, but you know anyway," she countered in her gebrocken English. "Because when you believe on it hard enough, it's going to happen."

"You think so?"

"I know it."

So as the sun settled behind the ridge line toward the Burrier farm, it became clear to me that we all live by different sets of rules. Sometimes they complement one another; sometimes they collide. The important thing is to stick to your own set. And no matter what rules you follow, Farmor was right. The future is definitely going to happen.

CHAPTER XVIII

To fly without wings, you must dream without limits.

When it was all over, I would write in my journal something to the effect that I would never forget those three memorable days. Of course, we've discussed at length how foolish such observations can be. We know what happens when time has a chance to toy with memories, to make an adjustment here, airbrush an image there, erase a detail or two. The passage of years alters recollections, often tying them up into tidier packages while dimming the crystalline clarity of the moment.

Naturally, my selective memory has chosen not to store every second of this major milestone of my 15th summer. But many vivid images remain, including the important ones, the ones that solidified the meaning of the hardboot rules, the ones that opened the door to at least a partial appreciation of life's glorious mysteries.

The regional pony club rally was a novel event for my friends and me. Though only a few years old, the national organization was growing rapidly in size and stature. The rally in Lexington would be the first major test for the local chapter, with nine teams from Ohio, Tennessee, Kentucky and Alabama competing for the regional championships.

We knew a lot of the kids from out-of-state, having competed against them at major horse shows in Louisville, Nashville or Cincinnati. We were accustomed to riding against each other and battling it out individually. But now, for the first time, we would be competing as teams, in an event where scores were combined and everyone's performance mattered. No one was quite sure how it would work. But the uncertainty lent an air of excitement to the event.

The rally was held on the sprawling Rodgers farm in western Fayette County, where volunteers had been busy for weeks setting up jumps, laying out dressage rings and arranging stabling on the grounds for two score horses. Each team was allocated four stalls and a tack room in one of the farm's classic broodmare barns. Colonel Rodgers even shipped a few of his own Thoroughbreds over to Keeneland to make room for the visitors.

On Thursday afternoon, I threw my clothes into a small suitcase, grabbed a tote bag that had been standing by my door for a couple of days, and went down to hook up with Far. We drove by the clinic for a quick check on Gray Smoke, whose leg was improving with each passing day, then headed out to the rally grounds, where I spent the afternoon putting last-minute coats of paint on tack boxes, rakes and pitch forks.

Everything had to be uniform. Each team had its own color combination to identify equipment. Every item had its designated place. All this was the stable manager's responsibility. This was my station, and I took it seriously.

Throughout the day, trailers rolled in and disgorged their loads of horseflesh. Competitors bustled back and forth, toting large trunks of equipment and constantly surrounded by chattering parents and coaches. One by one, my teammates made their appearance. As they unloaded and saw to their mounts' essential needs, I helped stow the gear in our designated tack room.

All the while, I kept an eye out for the Cerillis' American Traveler. The hours passed quickly as I hustled around the barns, trying to make myself useful. When I finally saw the silver-green trailer pulling into the stable area, I felt a frog vault into my throat. I gulped and continued the chores, trying to be cool, prepared for any calamity.

But she didn't disappoint me. Within minutes she popped around the corner of the shed row.

"Hi there," she beamed.

"Hi, Anna."

"We're over in that next barn," she pointed.

"I know." I had known for hours where she would be stabled. "Your horse ship over all right?"

"Yes. He's fine. But we've still got equipment to unpack. Just wanted to say hello."

My face felt like it was frozen. I forced out as broad a smile as I could. "I'm really glad you did," I said. "Because I've got something for you." Without waiting for her response, I dashed to the tack room, and fetched my tote bag.

"A promise is a promise," I said, handing over the peace offering.

One by one, she pulled the items out: a box of popcorn, a Coke, a package of milk duds, and a little silver horse head charm. As she exposed the gifts, her face wrinkled with delight. "You remembered!" she laughed.

"Of course."

Then, in one of those vividly cherished moments, she threw her arms around my neck and gave me a quick peck on the cheek.

"Thank you," she said. "Bye now."

She was running across the yard before I could recover. I just stood there with a stupid look on my face, and a warm tingle on my cheek.

"Bye," I mumbled, too low for anyone to hear. But it didn't matter. At that particular moment, nothing really mattered.

— • —

The event was a swirl of movement, to and from the grounds, in and out of barns, flying without wings over fences and running across fields with forgotten stock pins. It was a social swirl, with youngsters and adults and animals all mixed together in a hectic community. For two days we rubbed elbows in friendship and gritted teeth in competition.

The teams were all lodged at the Campbell House Inn on Harrodsburg Road. Some groups checked in as early as Wednesday and spent the extra time getting their horses used to the surroundings and visiting with family and friends. But by Thursday evening, parents were banned from the stables as well as team quarters at the hotel, and pony club chaperons took charge. There was an official post-dinner orientation, then everyone was sent off for a good night's sleep before the games began.

Naturally, Jack and I bunked together, having lucked into a nice room adjacent to the indoor pool, which we barely had time to enjoy. In fact, I didn't even dip a toe in it until late Saturday night when a certain redhead pushed me in. But I'm getting ahead of myself again...

After the organizers made their final room check, we enjoyed a last soft drink and thought about the day ahead.

Team at Pony Club rally

"You nervous?" Jack asked.

"Not really. We'll do fine."

"You sorry you won't be riding?"

I pondered this for a moment. "In a way, I guess. But I'm OK with it. I just have to do my part. That's what the rules require. If life gives you lemons, you make lemonade. If you have a mudder, you wait for rain."

"Spoken like a true hardboot."

"Naaeeh. Just a realist."

There was a short silence.

"Looks like you and Anna are finally hitting it off all right."

I probably blushed a little, but Jack couldn't tell in the dim light. "Yep. It took some time for us to get our signals straight. I guess girls can be funny that way. Seems a lot easier to communicate with horses."

Sprawled on his bed, Jack chuckled. "I know what you mean," he said. "One minute they're all smiles and sparkle, next minute they're distant as a mirage."

Somehow I knew he was thinking about Cathy May. In the interest of diplomacy, I decided to drop the subject.

"By the way, Jack..." I began.

"What?"

"Farmor says we're gonna win this thing."

"She does?!"

"Yep."

"What does she know about it?"

"Not much, maybe. But I think she may be onto something."

"Thought you said you were a realist."

"I am. But there's nothing wrong with dreams. So I'm putting all my faith in you."

He chuckled again. "Thanks for nuthin.'"

⊣ • ⊢

As we drifted off to sleep, I found myself wondering whether I cared about winning the rally. Winning isn't everything, Far always said. And the summer had surely put a lot of things in perspective. Considering the disappointment I had witnessed the past couple of months, a mediocre showing at the rally wouldn't matter much. Besides, our team winning would mean that Anna's team lost. That was an oddly disturbing thought, too.

But when push came to shove, I did want to win. Not because winning mattered, but because doing my best mattered. Not because I had to be best, but because the horse life required it of me. Was I really a hardboot? Maybe. Maybe not. But growing up amid hooves and fetlocks and withers and polls and muzzles and brushes and chestnuts had definitely made me who I was. And I was here to compete. The herd expected nothing less. Win or lose, they would give their all. The least I could do was follow suit.

Why were we here? Jack might have asked.

To follow the herd. To give them their due.

On the cross country course

The next forty-eight hours literally whizzed by, with little chance for reflection or savoring. Friday morning the teams were herded into a meeting room at the hotel for the written test. For an hour everyone scribbled frantically, trying to answer questions like: What is moon blindness? What is a bog spavin? When is linseed oil an appropriate feed supplement? There was even a question I recognized from Far's AG 131 exam: What is the average hay and grain requirement for a stabled adult horse?

Fifteen years at the riding academy had taught me this stuff. I felt good as I put down my pencil and handed in the test.

Then it was off to the event grounds. We had an hour to muck out, re-bed stalls and spruce up before a formal inspection of the stables, with each team graded on cleanliness and neatness. The teams stood at the ready while dour-faced grown-ups poked through straw to find missed clumps of manure or lifted saddle skirts looking for dirt. They inspected water buckets and feed tubs, bits and martingales, curry combs and sweat scrapers. When they left our area without assessing any demerits, we shared a quiet cheer.

The cross-country competition was held that afternoon. Coley, Macy, Jack and Rab trooped dutifully off to negotiate a strenuous two-mile course over 18 fences and through two farm ponds. One by one they returned, a little somber maybe, sweaty and splattered, but not visibly shaken. No falls. A couple of refusals at the imposing pile of logs. "Lots of people will have trouble at that jump," Macy assured us. "One guy from Northern Alabama got so disoriented there that he went off course," she related. Forgot to keep red on right, I chuckled. As team captain, Macy offered encouragement. "We can do it," she said. "Everybody concentrate."

So I did my part. Our barn was spotless. When a horse came in, he was untacked, sponged and cool-walked immediately. My ears pricked at the sound of manure dropping on straw. Within seconds the offending detritus was whisked away. Whenever a horse headed out, he was groomed and combed to a perfect gleam, his tack glistening with saddle soap and metal hardware sparkling in the August sun.

As the first day came to an end, we were spent, as much from excitement as physical exhaustion. We gathered in the hotel lobby just long enough to digest the standings. The cumulative scores, combining written tests, inspections and cross-country, were tight. Not more than forty points separated the top five teams: Middle Tennessee, Keeneland II, Keeneland I, Miami Valley and Northern Alabama.

We were in third place. The leading Tennessee team had excelled in the written test and been solid in the cross-country. Our friends on Keeneland II had done almost as well.

Before heading off to the team dinner and bed, I drew some satisfaction from the individual results on the written exam. Two people had perfect scores; an Alabama girl named Morris and yours truly. Unfortunately, the same couldn't be said of my teammates.

It was barely nine o'clock when Jack and I stretched out on our hotel beds.

"Third place?" Jack said. "I thought we'd done pretty good. I thought I did better on the written test."

"That's all right. We'll catch up."

"You sure. You still believe what your Grandmother said?"

"Tough competition," I replied. "That Nashville team looks sharp. And our own second team's no slouches."

"Especially that Cerilli girl, huh?"

I tried to ignore him. "We'll do better tomorrow."

Jack nodded, then after a pause added, "Pretty hectic schedule. Doesn't leave much time for socializing."

I knew full well what he was referring to. "I said hi to her at breakfast," I assured him.

"Glad to hear it. Wouldn't want our stable manager to be distracted."

"I'll be on guard."

"Good," Jack muttered. "Plenty of time for that later."

"Uh, huh," I agreed. I was in no hurry. There were no empty spaces in the pit of my stomach. I could wait.

⊣ • ⊢

Day Two proved no less frenetic, no less suspenseful. Dressage in the morning. Stadium jumping in the afternoon.

Stable duties kept me in the barn area. But my teammates reported back regularly. Our captain turned in a dynamite dressage round. Coley followed with a solid round. Jack was next, and I caught up with him as he headed out.

"Knock 'em dead," I urged, stroking Cavalier's shining buckskin coat.

"I've figured it out." Jack smiled back. "I'll just pretend I'm on Gay Blade."

"No. Cav's got it in him. Just tell him the herd is watching."

"Fair enough," Jack replied. As he gathered up his reins, he turned to me again. "Sometimes you're not as dumb as you look," he said.

Jack did us proud. I'm sorry I missed it. I would have loved to have seen that buckskin turn in the dressage round of his life. But I heard about it from the others. "What a ride!!" Rab exclaimed. "I've never seen that horse move so well!" Macy gushed. Jack himself returned to the barn area with only the slightest hint of smugness pasted on his face.

"How'd you do?" I asked.

"Not too bad," was his response as he patted Cavalier's neck. "I think he just pretended you were riding him."

But our euphoria was short-lived. Minutes later, Rab was in the barn area sounding the competitive alarm. "Keeneland II is still leading with one rider each to go," he announced. "Anna Cerilli just posted the highest individual score yet."

I wished I had seen that, too. But I heard about it later. My gutsy little redhead had put her tall gelding immaculately through his motions. "One of the nicest "C" level rides I've ever seen," Far commented. No faint praise from a master who had seen thousands.

— • —

So it all came down to the stadium jumping. The Keeneland teams were neck and neck. Only a few points separated them, points that could be lost on a single refusal or a couple of knock-downs. Thanks to a brace of mediocre dressage rounds, Middle Tennessee had fallen behind. But not too far. They still posed a challenge. Nor was the Northern Alabama team, reputed to have the best show jumpers in the South, out of it. In short, it was still anybody's championship.

At some point that afternoon, I was left alone in the barn area. I felt a certain incipient nervousness, mostly on behalf of my teammates. They had worked hard, trained hard, ridden hard. And in the heat of the competition, my will to win was surging. And off across the yard, I saw Anna come and go from the ring, poised so naturally in the saddle, a small girl on a big horse that still looked as if they belonged together. I smiled to myself, proud and happy and knowing what anticipation felt like.

I tried to refocus, to concentrate. I still had a job to do, I chastised myself. Seizing pitchfork and rake, I did yet another round of the stalls, picking a fresh pile from Cavalier's and removing stray strands of hay from a water bucket. Then, before hanging the equipment back up, I carefully extricated straw from the ends of the pitchfork.

At that moment, a gaggle of adults appeared, carrying clipboards and wielding pens. There were four of them, all sporting the official organizers' shirt. It was a surprise inspection team.

I stifled a gasp, then stood nervously by as they made their rounds, once more checking stalls and shed row and tack room. They conversed quietly as they worked, out of earshot. In a matter of minutes it was over, and without much more than a quick wave, they headed for the next barn.

I stood by the tack room for a moment, quelling a wave of panic. Had they found anything amiss? Was everything in order? But I couldn't see anything out of place and gradually, the feeling passed. I had done my best, I told myself. If this isn't good enough, what could possibly be better? Down the hall, a horse nickered agreement.

I took a deep breath and picked out the hints of hay, leather, manure and equines in the air. My eyes gathered in the summer sky and the barn turrets and a flight of swallows skimming treetops on the horizon. I suddenly felt enormously content. In that moment, the events of the summer coalesced. The lessons came together. All the things I had experienced merged. All the realizations. I had learned to be patient, to be aware of differences. I had learned the puzzling nuances of communication, that strong emotions can cloud judgment. I had learned about weaning and maturing and caring.

But most of all, I had learned about me, that there were so many dreams ahead, that life would offer profound sadness and incredible joy, and that my definition of winning might be a little different from anyone else's.

⊣ ● ⊢

In many ways, the banquet that night was something of a denouement. Macy, Coley, Rab and Jack had pulled it off, managing four of the top eight rounds in stadium jumping. And the kids in Keeneland II had done what they could, with Anna Cerilli turning in another perfect round. When the scores from the jumping were added, there were still only a couple of points difference, points that this time fell — just barely — in our team's favor. At the banquet tables, the conversation was cheerful, enthusiastic. There was good-natured ribbing. There were elaborate descriptions of this jump or that horse or that water bucket spilling on the district commissioner. There was no rancor, no envy.

After dinner, when the awards were announced, the teams were all seated together, the five of us in Keeneland I at one table and our five rivals from Keeneland II at the next. Though Anna and I sat with our backs to each other, she repeatedly tapped me on the shoulder to share some story or joke.

I felt great. But even though we knew what the final results would be, we still harbored some suspense, some sense of excitement at the finality of the formal announcement.

Ironically, the organizers stumbled, temporarily casting a serious chill on the proceedings. The president of the local Pony Club began his presentation by announcing that the final scores had been altered based on the results of a surprise inspection of the stable area. These inspections had resulted in demerits being assessed on Keeneland II and Middle Tennessee, he said.

"The scores have been calculated together with all other events," he boomed, "and the final standings are..."

A hush fell over the room. I felt the blood drain from my head. I looked over at the next table and caught Anna's eye. She managed a wan smile.

"In first place: Keeneland ONE."

Everyone at my table jumped up, screaming with joy. Everyone except me. I was still wondering.

"Second place: Middle Tennessee!"

No, I protested. It can't be. They were behind by at least 20 points!

I looked again at Anna. She was staring at her plate, any semblance of mirth totally stripped from her face.

"Anna," I called.

She didn't look up.

It was either instinct or habit that drove me to abandon the table and seek out Far in the crowded banquet room, the trusted man who could always fix things, always right a wrong, always comfort a hurting son or hurting yearling.

When I found him, at a side table with Mor and Vera, he was wearing his signature frown.

"There's something wrong," I pleaded. "They've calculated the scores wrong."

"Maybe," he said quietly.

I was taken aback. "But...but aren't you going to do something?"

He looked me squarely in the eye, with the faintest of smiles. "This isn't something for you or me to do," he said. "If there's a problem, it will be taken care of. Just leave it for now."

For a split second, I couldn't believe what I was hearing. For the shortest moment, I thought Far had failed me. And then I realized something quite different. He hadn't failed me at all. To the contrary, he was strengthening me. He was weaning me, cutting me loose from dependence on him, on the comforting expectations of childhood, on blind faith in authority, on philosophies that deny error. Moreover, he was, true to himself, once again counseling patience.

I hurried back to the team tables, and went straight to Anna's side. She looked up with a continued air of bewilderment.

"They'll get it straightened out," I assured her, trying to be supportive, perhaps sounding more confident than I was. "It'll work itself out."

In the background, the president was still announcing placings and awards. His voice reverberated heavily through the room.

"And now...for individual best combined score, "C" level."

We turned to listen...

"Miss Anna Cerilli, Keeneland Two!"

Before I knew it, she was in my arms. Right there in front of the whole horse world of the Bluegrass, crying and laughing and choking from joy and relief and confusion. I managed to hold her, awkwardly I'm sure, carefully I remember. She hugged me and pressed her head against my chest, muffling the many sounds her body was making. Then she quickly let go and sprinted to the podium to get her julep cup.

— • —

She came back, of course. All I had to do was wait right there. And the problem with the scores was finally resolved. Someone had written "100" instead of "10." Keeneland Two had been assessed ten demerits... for straw stuck on a pitchfork.

— • —

Boots off

Later that evening we danced. All the panic and anxiety began to fade, replaced by warmer and stranger emotions. At some point in the evening, I held Anna by the waist and lifted her into the air. She was so light; her waist as thin as a wasp's. I opened my lungs and shouted joyfully into the chords of a band somewhere in the room playing a song by the Imperials.

For the moment, I put my hard boots away.

Postscript

ost of this tribute to the horse world of my youth was written
more than a decade ago. Much has changed since then. The
medium-sized college town that once was Lexington, Kentucky, has
morphed into a sprawling regional hub of 300,000 people. Nonetheless,
the place clings fervently to its title as "Horse Capital of the World." And
the landscape around the ubiquitous housing developments is still dotted
with magnificent horse farms. The spring and fall meets at Keeneland
remain the social highlights they always were, and the sales sessions still
provide the best free entertainment in the Bluegrass. The Lexington Junior
League Horse Show is now in its 81st year. In southern Fayette County,
along the Kentucky River Palisades, the Iroquois Hunt Club continues
its century-long tradition of fine horsemanship, and local chapters of
the United States Pony Club continue to nurture future hardboots.

Yet so many of the people who grace these pages are gone. Far passed
away, on the farm with his boots nearby, as early as 1982. Both Farfar and
Farmor died in Norway in the 1970s. Lars LaCour and his gregarious
wife, Gunvor, are no longer with us, having lived their last years in
retirement in a charming lakeside cottage in rural New York state. Indeed,
Clovelly Farms no longer exists as the property was sold after the death
of its British owner, Robin Scully. Others who have slipped this mortal
coil include Dr. Bob Hensley, William Shorter, who went on to manage
Mill Ridge Farm and was at one time president of the Thoroughbred
Farm Managers Club, and Fauntleroy Pursley, master of the Iroquois
hounds for 40 years.

Marshall is gone, too, although his liver held out longer than anyone might have expected. He spent most of the 1980s in pleasant retirement until his heart stopped one evening as he sat in the shade of his front porch in Little Georgetown.

Mor, on the other hand, remains active, energetic and in great health. I firmly believe she will outlive us all. My sister, too, keeps her vocal chords in shape, having transitioned from the Handel-Haydn Society, the oldest professional chorus in the United States, to the Cantilena chorus. Both live in the Boston area.

Some of the old buddies are still around. Rab works as an editor and sportswriter in Lexington, and Coley runs a farm construction company in central Kentucky. Drew Thornton, our mercurial riding pal, met a stranger fate. He parachuted to his death in the Smokies with duffel bags of smuggled dope strapped to his body. Mason Winn married a Kiwi and went off to run a horse and sheep operation down under.

The star-crossed love of Melissa and Randy is the author's invention. Randy is a composite of the many stable managers who helped Far through the years. I learned many critical life lessons from them and remember them all fondly. One of them did accidentally shoot a horse while hunting rats, and the remorse he showed, as well as Far's calm forgiveness, are experiences I shall always admire.

Melissa, too, is purely fictional, although I have drawn freely upon the life of Pamela Brown, a matchless beauty who was a frequent visitor to our riding academy. Brown was only 28 years old when she and her husband crashed during an attempt to cross the Atlantic Ocean in a hot air balloon.

Of course, the school horses are enjoying greener pastures. One by one, they grazed their way into memory. A couple met accidental deaths, a couple were felled by severe colic or twisted intestines. Viking never recovered from an impacted tooth, and Lieutenant's heart gave out in the final stretch of a flat race at the Iroquois Point-to-Point. But most enjoyed a placid existence until old age caught up with them. Several, including Skew and Dancer and Colpin, were taken home by students at the riding academy who just couldn't live without them. The girls would cry until Daddy relented, and the horse would be shipped off to a pampered life on ten or twenty acres in Scott or Woodford County.

The wonderful gray horse with the bullet in his leg recovered just fine, and went on to become a family pet for a Lexington doctor and his wife.

Svart'n went to a summer riding camp in Shelby County. I visited him once after he'd spent several years there. He must have been at least twenty years old by then, but he still recognized me, whinnied and came galloping across the paddock to greet me.

Among the last to go was Queet'n. He graced the fields at Twin Brook Acres until the early 1990s, a treasured friend, gentle with children, reluctantly dutiful with adults. His clouded right eye always made me think of Marshall.

Jack desCognets is a fictional character, although some of my close friends might see parts of themselves in him. I would like to assure them that any negative aspects of the character were surely drawn on someone else.

And finally, Anna Cerilli is also drawn entirely from my imagination. There really never was anyone quite like her. Although, if there had been, I like to think she would still be surrounded by horses, maybe somewhere in the Midwest, in a place with horse-crazy kids trying to learn the hardboot rules. And occasionally, she might even think back on that memorable summer when we all set off on the rocky path to understanding.

—Dag Ryen

Santa Fe, New Mexico

July, 2017